Wokeistan: A Novel

Written by Tony DiGerolamo and Christian Beranek

South Jersey Rebellion Productions

First Edition: July 2019

Published in Laurel Springs, NJ by South Jersey Rebellion Productions

Library of Congress Reference Number: 1-7786231821

Version 1.0

Special thanks to: Adam Beranek, Beryl Beranek, Nick DiGerolamo, Steven DiGerolamo, Corey Sosner

Table of Contents

The Press of New York: January 20, 2021

Washington D.C.: Cold. Rainy. Miserable. These were the words that described the second inauguration of Donald J. Trump. Despite all the lies, all the investigations, all the outrages--- He's still the President of the United States.

"I'm lost!" screeched Amy, 22, from Columbus Ohio. "How did we let this happen? My country is gone!"

Members of the Resistance, once energized and fueled by rage, are tired of the fight. D.C. police came out in record numbers to control the streets, but Anti-Trump protesters seemed to have no stomach for battle four years later. The mood was as dreary as the weather. Riot police with shields, batons and helmets loomed over the young faces that were marching for a Democracy they may have lost forever.

"Trump has won," commented a despondent member of Antifa (the anti-fascist group that has been instrumental in battling the rise of the Right). "Congress won't impeach. It's time to impeach them. It's time to impeach the whole Electoral System."

Law enforcement blocked attempts by the protesters to disrupt the proceedings at every turn. Four years prior, the crowds had smashed windows and sets fires. This time, they were hesitant and afraid of the consequences. The Resistance knew that going to jail in Trump's America had become a bigger risk.

But amongst the somber marchers, there was hope.

Penny, a freshman at Upstate College, continued to lead chants of "Two-four-six-eight! We don't want your fascist hate!" with fervor. A few of the other marchers, inspired by her spirit, joined in.

"I'm just not going to give up against racism and fascism," Penny insisted as she marched along holding up a sign that said #NotMyPresident.

4

"We're the people and the people want Trump gone! If he won't go, we're going to make him go, okay? Because, I don't have to take this!"

As long as bright, young activists like Penny still exist, perhaps there is a sliver of hope for this once proud and free country...

Chapter 1

Dr. Lawrence F. Mondel loved certain things. He loved his daughter, he loved the Mets, he loved a good whiskey, he loved books by Solzhenitsyn, and quite possibly his ex-wife a few years ago. But his one true love, the immutable thing in his life which he had never soured on, was the college campus that had made his life what it was today, Upstate College.

Upstate College was a small liberal arts school just off the Finger Lakes in the middle of New York. As the second semester of 2021 started, the air was brisk and full of possibilities. It was impossible for him to contain his enthusiasm. Molding young minds was a fascinating enterprise, especially as a Political Science Doctor.

Many of his students had just returned from Trump's re-election inauguration so they would be primed for discussing the protest, the politics and the future. With a president like Trump and a polarized electorate, it was a political junkie's dream of constant political debate. While most people had soured on the mere mention of such a discussion, Mondel thrived on his students' fiery political rhetoric.

Mondel struggled to balance his coffee cup between his briefcase and his mouth as he slid out of his 2013 sedan. He stood upon the well-salted faculty parking lot and kicked his door shut behind him. Then, taking control of the coffee cup again, he put his briefcase at his side and looked up the Upstate College Admissions Hall.

Walking past the building, he caught a glimpse of himself in the reflection of the dark glass of the hall. He remembered doing the same thing when he and his father had taken the campus tour back in the late 90's. The doctor looked quite a bit like his father at 45: salt and pepper black hair on a round head, beard, glasses, brown leather jacket over a button down shirt and creased slacks.

He was reasonably fit again, thanks to his divorce of two years ago. Brianna was in Binghamton with Zoe. Even though he couldn't see "Little Z" as often as he liked, he had come to terms with that. Quite frankly, it was a relief not to have his daughter see him try to date, even though he was making inroads.

"Morning Tabitha," Mondel greeted the adjunct professor in the hallway.

"Just dropped off those updated syllabi," she informed him. "I'll be assisting Professor Martinez if you need anything."

"Excellent," noted the doctor continuing toward the office. "Thank you much."

He entered the faculty offices which hadn't moved since his student days.

"Morning, Dana," Mondel greeted the faculty secretary.

"Hey, doc," she smiled. "Professor Papadopoulos said to tell you he'll see you at the Faculty Mixer tonight. Here's your mail."

"Thanks."

Mondel walked past the horseshoe-shaped receptionist desk and toward the offices behind it. In the old days, the place seemed to be covered with post-it notes, file folders, stacks of books and other papers. In the Internet Age, the faculty offices had been stripped of that clutter. He couldn't help but note that the space seemed a little more sterile having lost its professorly allure.

His own office did have some of that clutter. There was a Mets mascot bobblehead his class gave him in '15. A few scholarly tomes were placed on the shelves. He hoped to inspire the students when they sat in the one extra seat just a few feet away. Out the window, past his laptop monitor and a framed selfie of himself with President Obama on the '08 campaign trail, he could see a group of dour freshmen walking across campus.

Many of the student body, especially the more politically inclined girls, had gone to the Womens' March and Trump's inauguration protest. The rainy, miserable weekend, he heard, had not gone well. He expected a lot of Trump rants in the group discussions on Thursday. Fortunately for the doctor, there was no Wednesday class. His day consisted mostly of organizing the student rolls and holding office hours. No one was going to see him on the second day back from Christmas Break.

Wes Conners popped his head through the doorway. Wes was a professor of chemistry in the Science Department and they became lunch buddies a few years ago when he joined the faculty. Jokingly referred to as Heisenberg for his resemblance to Walter White from Breaking Bad, Wes had become a good friend during the dark days of the divorce.

7

"Hey, bro. What's good?" he greeted. "We on for lunch? Where you wanna go?"

"Any place with a salad bar," responded Mondel.

"Ah, you're no fun since you started dating again," he teased. "What happened to that foodie who used to pound down burgers while cursing his ex?"

"I've actually had a couple of dates, so…"

"Good for you, man. Is this Celia? From the art department?"

"Theater department," Mondel corrected.

"Am I going to have to hang out at the faculty thing by myself?"

"Ah, it's nothing official. Only a few dates. Wouldn't call us an item yet."

"Yet? Look at you! So goddamned hopeful. You make me sick! Congrats, buddy."

"Thanks. How are the students?"

Wes exhaled and laughed.

"Jesus Christ," he said shaking his head and lowering his voice. "They're bitching about Trump in **my** class, so you know they're wound up this year! I don't know how you stand it. My brother used to come back from Brown pissin' and moanin' about Reagan and I wanted to shoot myself!"

"You know, they're just kids trying to figure things out," smiled Mondel. "Hopefully they'll vent and then go back to thinking."

"Be prepared for a lot of venting!" Wes assured. "I'll see you at one."

The Faculty Mixer was held at the Dean's residence just down the road from the college, promptly at 7pm. The three foot stone wall topped with four feet of wrought iron spikes, gave the house a mansion-like façade. The entire faculty would be there to eat, drink, catch up, network— But mostly complain.

"Thank Christ I'm out before this Quad Class bullshit kicks in," Professor Papadopoulos said gesturing with his highball. "'The fuck Albert thinks he can do combining curriculums across departments? Rather get butt raped by a salami."

Professor P was a 70-something poly-sci chair with white hair, dated suit and an always salty attitude. It was never bitter. He had a kind of playfulness in the way he tossed out the most vulgar metaphors he could think of.

Standing next to him laughing was Wes, who never tired of the act. Also nearby was Diana Martinez. Diana was part of the Poly-Sci Posse, a 50-ish bookish woman who adored Professor P almost as much as Mondel did. She'd been blushing at his jokes since she met him as a freshman.

8

Next to her was Mel Franklin. He was a quiet, squat fellow that kept to himself. Mondel maybe exchanged a total of 200 words with him over the four years that they had worked together. He taught himself almost as much as he taught his students, pouring over books online and in the real.

Hovering nearby trying to be a part of the scene was Mike Fawkes, also one of the posse. Fawkes was only 38 and still looked like one of the students. Hired on staff because of the reams of recommendations he got coming out of Berkeley, Professor P had quickly cut him down to size for being the mental midget he actually was. Mondel grabbed a drink and joined them.

"Lawrence," greeted Professor P as if scolding him. "You made it here like you made it to my class. Late. Where the fuck have you been? Trying to get your balls back from your wife? Too late now!"

"Hey, Professor P," Mondel replied with a smile. "It's your last Faculty Mixer or last chance to quit."

"Quit? Nah, fuck quitting. I wouldn't give these cocksuckers the satisfaction. I'm going to take them for all the retirement pay I can," responded the prof, twirling his ice. "You poor bastards don't get half the bells and whistles I do."

"We'll miss you, boss," Diana added. "Who is going to tell students to go fuck themselves now?"

"You, Diana, you!" Professor P joked poking a finger at her. "You can do it! Just let the darkness and bile guide you, girl!"

The group laughed and it was all in good fun. Fawkes, as always, had somehow not gotten the read of the room.

"The college should give us a retirement package comparable to yours. It should all be the same," Fawkes suggested. "Adjusted for the standard of living, of course."

The needle skipped off the record. Professor P was barely tolerating him.

"Hey, Fawkes, pull Karl Marx's dick out of your mouth for ten seconds and go get me another drink, huh?" suggested the prof.

"Sure, thing," the young professor said, off to get him another highball.

The group held their laughter until he walked away and then snickered.

"There he goes, ladies and gentlemen," said P condescendingly. "The most published Master's student at Berkeley."

"Is that why the Dean hired him?" asked Wes.

"Yeah, he was billed as having a massive intellectual cock," explained P. "Turns out, it's just an inflated resume jammed down the front of his pants. Albert would've been better off hiring a fucking photocopier. It would've produced better papers and acted more intelligent."

"At least I won't have to cross-combine a class with him," Mondel noted.

"God speed, Wes," Professor P quipped. "You'll be teaching Communism on the Periodic Table before you know it."

"Good Christ!" laughed Wes.

"He's not joking," Diana added.

"Mel, try to let the rest of us get in a fucking word once in a while," said the professor, trying to draw him out.

"Sorry. Thinking about this Foucault book I'm reading," Mel mumbled, checking his watch. "Excuse me."

Mel headed for the bathroom. He'd skip out shortly after the Dean spoke, not even saying goodbye. Franklin's social skills were as withered as the ivy on the side of the school in the winter.

The Dean entered the room and clinked his glass with a spoon to get everyone's attention. Dean Albert Metuchen was a pleasant administrator who excelled at throwing mixers. The booze was always top shelf, the food was always great and the light jazz was tuned to just the right volume. His soft, doughy face smiled at the gathering. For him, this was the culmination of the year. He had pushed hard for increased enrollment to replace the students who left after the first semester. The budgets, the hiring of staff, the project to expand the campus and even the landscaping did not escape his notice. When summer break came, the Dean would be winding up again to prep for Fall 2021.

"Everyone, thanks for coming," the Dean grinned. "We had a wonderful first semester and I expect a wonderful second semester. This is technically Upstate's 79th year in service to the community. Please be extra sensitive to the students this week. I'm sure you can understand they've all been triggered by the re-election of the president."

"Boo-booooo," muttered one of art professors.

A low ripple of laughter echoed through the room as Fawkes came back with Professor P's drink. Mondel turned and spotted Celia Lilywater standing with the theater and art department. He made eye contact and toasted her. She toasted back and smiled.

"She's cute," Professor P muttered under his breath. "Just remember your Proust. Theater girls get wet for that."

Lawrence shook his head. Even now, the old professor knew how to embarrass him.

"Here's to another safe and productive semester at Upstate," the Dean toasted.

The room returned the gesture and the mixer continued. Mondel and P stood apart from the other teachers talking privately.

"Seriously, I hope it works out," Professor P added. "You deserve it, Lawrence."

"What about you? Make any headway in that area?" asked Mondel.

"Not yet," P said, looking down into his drink somberly. "Robert's been gone eight years now? His death was the hardest thing to deal with, next to retiring."

"You sound like they're going to seal you up in a mausoleum."

"Aren't they?"

"Take some time. Write your book. Then you can do what Roger Greizer's doing— Going from campus to campus giving talks and doing signings," Mondel suggested.

"You always had good ideas, Lawrence, I'll give you that," admitted P. "But the world's changed."

"It's what it's always been," Mondel concluded. "Bright eyed students get to meet wise author who comes to the college to give a talk."

"Uh-huh," the professor said skeptically. "What's the book?"

"The Centrist's Handbook. What? It's not like he's a Republican."

"No, a centrist is worse to these people. They're going to eat him alive."

Chapter 2

At class the next morning, Mondel wasted no time discussing the reading assignment. He wanted to make it clear that Poly-Sci 101 didn't stop just because you went to D.C. for a protest. A little fear motivated the students. He was still trying to wake their brains up from the high school drudgery they had memorized from rote. They were just starting to get interesting at the end of class.

"But I thought we lived in a democracy," said Kyle Vivaldi, posing a non-question question.

"It's a Democratic Republic," corrected Mondel. "A straight democracy would be vulnerable to the tyranny of the majority."

"Yeah, see that's what I don't get," Tynesha Adams added. "How can it be a tyranny if it's a democracy? You're voting."

"Imagine if this class was just a straight democracy," Mondel taught. "Now we get together and vote to take your money and distribute it to the rest of the class."

"Whoa. No-no," laughed Tynesha.

"You're out-voted," shrugged Mondel. "Ben Franklin said democracy is two wolves and a sheep voting on what's for dinner."

The class was amused by that analogy and Mondel prepared to move on. But as he turned to walk back to the front of the classroom, a student spoke.

"But what if distributing her money to the rest of us is the right thing to do?" she asked.

Mondel turned. Sitting in the back of the room was a freshman girl with multi-colored hair, a denim jacket with too many pins, glasses and a pudgy face.

"I'm sorry," said Mondel not remembering her name. "Gina?"

"I go by G. Just the letter G," she corrected. "If Tynesha has too much money, why shouldn't the rest of us get a share? That's fair."

"Uh, because who are you to take her money?" Mondel said, mildly incredulous. "That would be stealing."

"If we voted on it, it would be legal," she pointed out.

"Maybe, but that doesn't make it ethical. Hitler was elected legally," Mondel pointed out. "And despite the fact that everything the Nazis did was technically legal, I don't think you'd call them fair."

The tone indicating the end of the class sounded.

"Next time," Mondel added, as the students left. "Don't forget, Roger Greizer is giving a talk on his book, The Centrist Handbook. Please come out. We'll be discussing it the next class."

"Will he be selling the books?" asked Tyler Brown. "Or do we have to buy it at the bookstore?"

"Bookstore unless you ordered one from Amazon, I'm afraid," Mondel told him.

As the class cleared out, G and her friend Penny stopped at his desk. Penny was a tall, skinny, blonde girl with an Elizabeth Taylor Cleopatra bob and combat boots. She had model good looks, but a dour spirit. Her t-shirt had the outline of a coat hanger and the words "Never Again".

"Dr. Mondel," Penny informed him. "We just want to let you know we're dropping your class."

"What? Why?" asked Mondel.

"We can't be a part of your class if you're going to support a fascist like Greizer," she said self-righteously.

"Fascist? If you think Greizer is a fascist, I don't think you understand what fascism means," Mondel said. "You two are bright, articulate--- I was looking forward to some great discussions with---"

"No," said Penny. "I have to go before I'm triggered."

G made eye contact but said nothing.

Judging by their early political leanings, the doctor figured they'd probably be more comfortable in another class. With Fawkes, they'd skate to an easy A.

Penny stomped toward the door indignantly. The sound of her combat boots reminded Mondel of soldiers marching. G slowly trailed after eyeing Mondel the entire way out of the room.

Jumping into the car, the doctor headed off campus. Upstate's college town was the kind of place that had one of everything: one supermarket, one diner, one department store, one hotel--- Since the town was kind of dreary, it did have plenty of bars. Most of the locals lived in residential communities away from the center. They avoided the college kids during the year.

The Commons, at the center, was considered almost an extension of Upstate. It held various vanity businesses belonging to the spouses of faculty and the administration. Brianna had talked about taking over the candle shop at one point. Mondel thanked God every day she had changed her mind. It was nothing but a money pit.

There were, of course, former students that had opened places the undergrads loved like Grenadine's Ice Cream Shop, Strictly Stombolis, Upstate Comics, Patchouli and Things and every kind of niche market thing you could think of. They'd do okay for a few years, limping along on the sales of fellow alumn, until those alumni graduated and they were left to fend for themselves.

Mondel was headed for the Upstate Downstairs Tavern & Grille. It was the typical lunch stop for faculty members since it was slightly high end. Despite being located at the edge of the Commons, you usually didn't run into students there.

The doctor left his car in a two level parking garage and walked to the ground floor. He spotted Homeless Vic immediately upon hitting the street. He pulled a couple of bucks from his wallet and handed it to him.

Vic was a spry, 40-something with gray hair and a scraggily beard. He looked a little like Garrett Morris in a stained overcoat. Vic had driven the other homeless guys away to get this primo spot. He was a veteran that probably deserved a whole lot better for his service.

"Hey Vic," he greeted.

"Dr. Mondel!" Vic said cheerfully. "How are you on this blessed day?"

"Good, you staying warm?"

"Thanks to people like you, I am!" he said gesturing to his begging cup.

Mondel went into the tavern and found Professor Papadopoulos at their usual booth. He didn't see anyone else with him.

"Where is everyone?" he asked.

"Wes had a department meeting and Diana had some kind of dust up with her students," he explained. "Which segues into why I should probably talk to you alone."

The waiter came by. Mondel ordered his lunch salad, but Professor P waved him off. This was unusual for him. He normally ate a big lunch or at least a Beef on Weck.

"What's on your mind?" replied Mondel, concerned.

"How much do you know about this Greizer fellow?"

"He's an author, political pundit---"

"Was he on Fox?"

14

"Maybe, I think he did all the big shows promoting his book. Why? What's going on?"

"Some of Diana's students had a meltdown when she mentioned Greizer to them. They're insisting he's some kind of far-right wingnut."

"That can't possibly be true," Mondel dismissed. "NPR talked about his book. I think he did an interview with Rachel Maddow."

"Look, these kids with helicopter parents shit their pants if you even say the word Republican around them," Professor P said. "You know I don't give a fuck about their tender sensibilities, but you know Albert hates controversy."

"I swear to you, this guy couldn't be less controversial!" Mondel laughed. "The name of his book **is** The Centrist Handbook."

"Well, look, do me a favor. Make sure you're there to hold the Millennial Babies hands," Papadopoulos requested. "The last thing I need is some lawsuit from a speaker if one of the kids takes a swipe at him."

"You're talking crazy, Professor," Mondel said incredulous. "He's not even a Republican and it's not even mandatory that they go!"

"Just make sure he gets in, promotes his book and he's on his way," Professor P instructed.

"We normally take the guest speaker out to dinner," Mondel reminded him.

"If you want to do that, I'm fine with it," the professor said. "But think how it will look to the cry baby fucktards in your class."

"I think they can handle it."

Professor P downed the rest of his drink, set the glass on the table and pushed it away.

"Didn't you have two kids drop Poly-Sci today?"

Mondel was caught. He didn't think Professor P would find out, let alone that quickly.

"True."

"Just be down there and keep a lid on things," he advised. "Here's some cash. Take Greizer to some place off campus. Some place a fucking student can't afford."

"What about the rich ones?" Mondel joked.

"Then they'll be conservatives and it won't matter," the professor responded, mildly worried.

"I think you're being paranoid."

"Lawrence, I don't need this bullshit in my last year. I'm trying to get into retirement mode. Do you read?" Professor P said, trying not to sound too annoyed.

"Yes, sir. I'm on it."

15

"Good lad," he complimented. "And on a personal note, if it wasn't for people like you and Diana--- Good people I know that can run the department--- I wouldn't be retiring. Probably just stay here to see if I can outlive Albert."

"I think you're good," the doctor replied confidently. "We're gonna be fine."

Mondel got back to the campus and called in before Dana left for the day. Greizer was already at the hotel, preparing for his 7pm talk. The doctor went down to Cicero Hall. The maintenance crew was setting up the room. It was led by Omar, a no-nonsense handyman with rough hands and a thick mop of black hair.

"Hey guys," the doctor greeted. "Everything okay for the talk tonight, Omar?"

"Yeah-yeah, sure doc," the handyman said, greeting him. "Why? Something wrong?"

"I don't think so, but the chair's worried the speaker might make some waves tonight," Mondel admitted. "If you want to limit access by keeping the doors on the left side of the room locked, I'm fine with it."

"Yeah, sure," Omar shrugged, not really understanding what the big deal was. "The students will have to walk all the way around to the front, but you're the boss."

"Thanks, Omar," Mondel said, keeping his voice low. "And let's just keep this between you and me, okay?"

"Sure," he agreed.

The situation would probably mean a lower turn out for Greizer, but if it deterred the students who didn't really want him on campus anyway--- It would be worth it.

By 6:45, the students were filling up some of the seats in the hall. It looked like a normal turnout, twenty or so interested souls and one or two big fans. He spotted Tyler from class.

"Hey, Tyler, thanks for coming out," Mondel said, relieved to see him.

"No problem, doc. I read most of Greizer's book. It's pretty interesting," Tyler said.

"Oh, you got a copy?"

"Actually, I downloaded a pirated Kindle version. Sorry. I just wanted to ask relevant questions."

"I won't tell if you won't," Mondel promised.

Mondel and Tyler shared a fist bump. Behind them, Greizer had arrived.

"Excuse me," said Mondel.

The doctor walked up to Greizer. He was wearing a hand-tailored suit and looked TV ready. He kind of resembled an older, version of Anthony Mackie, but with a bald head and thick mustache.

"Hello, Dr. Mondel," he greeted in his deep, confident baritone. "Thanks for hosting this."

"We're honored to have you," Mondel smiled.

"This is a beautiful campus," he complimented. "A bit far out in the woods for me though. I graduated from Syracuse."

"Go Orange Men," Mondel said. "There are bottles of water at your podium and if there's anything else you need, just let me know."

"I will," he assured.

Mondel sat in the back of the room, while Greizer got himself situated on stage. He had brought a handful of books. He wasn't supposed to sell them directly, but typically colleges looked the other way.

As Greizer prepared, Mondel heard some of the students try the locked doors on the left side of the hall. The noise of the people pulling on the other side wasn't loud enough to alert the other students in the room.

Greizer was already making small talk from the stage as he was setting up.

"Mr. Greizer, do you represent a particular party?" asked one of the students in the front row.

"No, political centrism tries to get beyond the tribalism and the ideologies that divide us," he explained, stacking his books.

"So it's about compromising the two positions?" asked Tyler.

"We'll get into it, but it's not so much about compromise," Greizer defined. "It's about using reason to pick the most pragmatic solution to the problem."

"But what if you have an unreasonable president?" asked one of the girls.

"Well, that's subjective, but I'll tell you what," he said checking his watch. "It's a little after seven so let's get into it."

Mondel looked around the room, everything seemed to be normal. Surely Professor P was just being overly cautious. He'd tease the old guy at lunch tomorrow about it.

"Democrats, Republicans. Liberals, Conservatives," Greizer began. "These are labels for some people, but what about the rest of us? What about the people that have nuanced positions? What about people--- Most people, who are Centrist? This is why I wrote The Centrist Handbook."

17

Suddenly, out of the corner of his eye, Mondel saw a student rushing to the locked doors. She pushed them open and a small throng of mostly girls entered. In the group, he recognized G and Penny.

"Oh, good, come right in," offered Grezier. "We're just getting started. As I was saying, most people are Centrist."

"Two-four-six-eight! We don't want your fascist hate!" Penny suddenly shouted.

The rest of the group started joining in the chant. A handful of the students in the audience now stood and joined in. Greizer looked bemused. Mondel broke out in a sweat.

"Two-four-six-eight! We don't want your fascist hate!" the group chanted.

"Whoa-whoa-whoa, now," Greizer said, now picking up the microphone and putting it close to his mouth so he could be heard. "I am not, nor have I ever been a fascist. Now I'm happy to have a dialogue with you and answer your questions, but I think you have me confused with someone else."

"Do you acknowledge the systemic misogyny and racism in our institutions?!" cried Penny.

Greizer couldn't believe he was getting the question. He looked out into the audience and made eye contact with Mondel. Was this a joke?

"Young lady," he said incredulous. "I'm a **black** man."

"Exactly!" said G, now springing her "trap". "A black **man**. You come in here and use a problematic term like 'black', when it's person of color. As a person of color, of African, Indigenous, Pan Asian and Muslim descent--- As an atheist and differently-abled person---"

"Wait, did you say Muslim-Atheist?" asked Grezier, confused. "How can you be a Muslim-Atheist?"

"Don't deny her personhood! Don't deny it!" screeched Penny. "Two-four-six-eight! We don't want your fascist hate!"

Greizer was reeling. He was astonished to be facing such a determined, hostile force for promoting a book about reasonable politics. He tried engaging the students, but they just weren't listening. Mondel rushed to the front of the stage and attempted to diffuse the situation.

"Calm down, everyone! Calm please!" Mondel shouted over the chanting. "Mr. Greizer is a guest of the department and he's come here to speak!"

"This is part of the Patriarchal construct that steals voices from women and people of color!" proclaimed Penny.

"You're not making any sense!" Tyler stood up and countered. "Can you please just be quiet for the speech?"

18

"Don't deny her agency!" insisted G.

"Her what?"

"Uh, it's called her **agency**, Tyler!" added a student condescendingly, as he taped the entire event on his phone while eating soy curls from a bag.

The heavyset speaker was a male student with glasses and a scraggily beard named Santos Ortez-Yama. He cheered on the girls. Santos had a reputation for being an activist on campus because he had been in a viral video where he kicked an abortion protestor. The woman ended up not pressing charges. Santos was wearing a t-shirt that said, "Men of Quality do not fear Equality".

Every word that came out of Greizer or Mondel's mouth was booed, while anything that came from the other side was immediately agreed with and cheered--- They could not agree with the mob fast enough.

"I am a person of color!" Greizer said in disbelief that he had to repeat it. "I understand the struggle!"

"You said you were a black **man**," repeated G. "Now you modified your words because you know you're wrong!"

"I'm not even here to speak about racial issues!" Greizer countered, not understanding why these students weren't getting this simple concept. "I'm here to promote my book and talk about Political Centrism!"

"That is **exactly** what the Nazis and fascists used to come to power!" G said sinisterly.

"What? No! That's not even close to being right!" Greizer said, shocked she would even suggest it.

"Exactly. We're not close to 'right'. We're far away from you alt-right types!" G pointed out, getting another round of applause.

"Look, if you'll just listen to what I have to say---"

"We don't **listen** to fascists! We deplatform them!" Penny proclaimed. "Two-four-six-eight! We don't want your fascist hate!"

Grezier moved away from his podium and gestured for Mondel to come up to the stage. He turned off his microphone.

"What the Hell have you gotten me into, Mondel?" Grezier demanded under his breath, starting to lose his temper. "Will you get these crazy bitches out of here?"

"Let me get Safety and Security on the phone," Mondel said, dialing the number on his cell. "I apologize. We'll get them calmed down and give you some more time."

Grezier attempted to go on with his talk, but the chanting kept drowning him out. Fifteen minutes later, a couple of uniformed security officers arrived and the mob started to boo them.

"What's the problem, doc?" one of the officers asked.

"These students won't allow our speaker to speak," explained Mondel.

"You bring in your goons, Mondel?" accused one of the girls. "We won't be bullied!"

Santos, who had winded himself and sat down, now struggled to get to his feet to defend the girls.

"Yeah, why don't you pick on a **man**? I-I-I'll bet you won't do **that**!" Santos stammered with a mouthful of chips. "I'll bet you won't pick on-on-on me!"

The officers walked past Santos and addressed Penny who they perceived as the leader of the group. Santos tried to get back in front of the officers, but he was afraid he might push one of them. He just ended up making an ineffectual attempt to climb over the auditorium seats to get back into their view while the officers talked.

"Look, if you're going to create a public nuisance, you'll be asked to leave," the lead officer stated.

"This isn't a public space!" G pointed out. "This is a private college that we pay for and we're not doing anything illegal!"

"Fascists! Fascists! Fascists!" shouted Penny, shortening the chant just to that.

Faced with an immutable wall of unreasonableness, the officers were unsure of how to proceed. They decided to check with their supervisor and when they left to do so, the mob prematurely cheered. Meanwhile, Greizer continued his talk as best he could under the circumstances. The audience had moved close to the stage and he was speaking to them without the microphone. He was telling them that the mob perfectly represented the extreme side of politics he was trying to warn against.

Mondel watched as G made the calculation. She nodded for the group to move close to the stage, right into Greizer's face and that of the students attempting to listen. Mondel tried to talk to them as they moved, but they just kept chanting.

"Why did you people come to college?" Greizer shouted over the chorus. "Was it just to scream at people?"

"Two-four-six-eight! We don't want your fascist hate!" shouted the mob.

While the security officers negotiated with their supervisor on what they may or may not do to students, Greizer continued to give his talk as best he could. Even with the protest in his face, he made some salient points about Centrism. The crowd was uninterested. When the clock hit eight, he thanked everyone and prepared to leave.

"You milquetoast fence sitter!" shouted Penny. "It's people like you that **didn't** stop the Holocaust!"

"I hope your parents realize that they're wasting their money on you!" he shouted to the mob. "Every day is an opportunity to learn, unless you act like this!"

Greizer was just about to leave when he gestured to the throng to make that point. Mondel would have been relieved to get him out of there, but then he saw the projectile. A milkshake, its lid coming lose, sailed over the crowd and hit Greizer. The milky, ice cream treat splashed his face, suit and pile of books. He finally lost his cool.

"Aw, what the fuck?!" he snapped.

The Safety and Security officers, now faced with an actual violation they could understand, pulled the student responsible out of the crowd. It was G. Grabbing her cane and grabbing her arms, the officers arrested her, much to the objection of the mob.

"No-no! Don't arrest her!" insisted Penny. "She hasn't done anything!"

"Arrest me!" Santos shouted, offering up his hands.

"She just hit that man with a milkshake!" said the lead officer ignoring him. "We all just saw it."

Greizer rushed outside and Mondel chased after him. He had a car that was waiting to take him back to his hotel.

"I am so sorry, Mr. Greizer," the doctor said, begging his forgiveness. "Let me make it up to you with a dinner. Completely on the college."

"If you don't mind, Dr. Mondel, I need to get the fuck out of here," Greizer told him, furious about the whole event. "Dinner's not going to cut it. I will send the college the bill for my suit. I don't know what you teach here, but it is some fucked up view of the world."

"We don't," assured Mondel. "These students--- This event was an aberration. Let me assure you. This is no fault of the curriculum."

"Isn't it?" asked Greizer seriously. "Let's go, driver."

As Greizer's car drove off, the officers took G to their cruiser. Inside Cicero Hall, the mob was throwing other food items and garbage from a trash can they knocked over. When Mondel came back into the room, they scattered. The auditorium was an absolute wreck.

A few minutes after the students left, Omar and the maintenance crew returned to the room. He was shocked at what happened. Mondel felt obligated to linger and explain to them the situation.

"Look, I'm sorry," Mondel offered. "I know it's late and you guys don't want to be cleaning, but we had an incident with the speaker."

"Jeez, doc, what's wrong with this speaker?" asked Omar.

"It wasn't him, it was the students," Mondel insisted.

Chapter 3

Hannah Miller, Olivia Ross, Alyssa Davis, Sofía Garcia, and several other girls gathered at the Student Union in the aftermath of the protest. It was a Mid-Century style building that had recently undergone a costly facelift. The renovation had barely been approved by the Board of Regents after a long battle. It wasn't a matter of how much money was to be spent, but which building was next-in-line to get the funds. Some pushed for the Welcome Center, as it was the face of the campus. However, an elite group of alumni who had fond memories of the Student Union were the deciding factor.

The Regents decided to keep most of its architectural design, complete with simple lines, floor to ceiling windows in front that spanned all five floors, and replacements for some of the original furniture. The new elements added were more seating areas and a complete tech overhaul. The new wifi system was blazing fast. Many students came to the Union to update their apps or upload large files for projects, all-the-while enjoying drinks and snacks from the franchise Seattle coffee chain that had moved into the old campus coffee shop's spot.

The coffee and the fast wifi were the main reason such an eclectic, seemingly disparate group of young female students found themselves hanging out in the lobby. There was a buzz of energy in the air, as if something could happen at any moment, but they stayed focused on their phones--- because to them, more was happening within those devices. Their eyes remained firmly fixed on their screens as they scrolled through Twitter. They searched for reactions to the short video clip of G throwing the milkshake that had just gone viral.

After some time, Hannah, a statuesque redheaded sorority sister with Omicron Pi Alpha, broke the silence. Her perfectly manicured bright red fingernails danced across the screen of her phone as she talked.

23

"Who was that girl?"

"They're calling her 'G'," Sofía said without looking up from her own phone.

"I know **that**," Hannah said in a dismissive tone. "But what's her story? She's a freshman?"

"Yeah. Tynesha said she quit Mondel's class today," Sofía explained.

"The hot Poly-Sci professor?" asked Oliva, the pixie-like sophomore holding a white chocolate mocha latte in a to-go cup.

"Gross," Hannah said.

"Well, I have a thing for older daddies," Olivia said with a coyish sip.

"That's disgusting."

"But not wrong," Olivia said, thus ending the debate. "I know a certain T.A. that's **very** not wrong, right Alyssa?"

Alyssa made a face, turned and saw Mia Ward walk into the lobby.

Mia was a junior majoring in Gender Studies with a focus on Third Wave Intersectional Feminism. She looked down at her phone as a text popped up. After reading it she looked over at Alyssa and shook her head. Alyssa was a senior studying Philosophy and barely spoke unless prodded to.

"I'm right here. Why didn't you call over?" Mia asked as she approached the group.

"I didn't want to seem overly aggressive," Alyssa explained. "Besides, texting is easier."

"What do you think about all of this craziness, Mia?" Hannah asked.

"Don't say the 'c' word," Alyssa said in what she considered a raised tone.

"Cunt?"

"No, that word is ok. The one you said before it, however. It's problematic."

"Fine. Mia, what do **you** think about all of this?"

"I think it's crazy," Mia said in a somewhat defiant manner.

Alyssa took note. Then, she went on the attack. She had been prodded, after all. "Third Wave Feminism is over, **Mia**."

"Don't give me that Fourth Wave nonsense, Alyssa. There is no such thing."

As the schism formed, Madeline, a trans girl, looked up from her phone and let out a shrill cackle. None of the other girls could ever get used to the noise she made when this happened, but had said nothing to her about it. To each other, however, when she wasn't around, it was the topic of much disdain and mean laughter.

"What is it?" Hannah asked.

24

"Check my YouTube channel. I edited some video together from the protest and it's gone viral!"

At that moment Penny strode by the outside windows, looked through them, saw the girls chatting while looking down at their phones. She then turned around to enter through the front doors, made a beeline to the group and planted herself in front of them.

"Greetings," she said.

Hannah sized her up and down, then looked over at Mia. Mia nodded back, then shifted her focus to the new girl.

"You're Penny, right? You were there when G walked out of Mondel's class?"

"We walked out, correct," Penny answered plainly.

"Why?"

"Mondel was spreading patriarchal fascist doctrine. We don't have to accept it."

"Uh, ok, I don't think that's---" Mia started before Hannah cut her off.

"You here to throw a milkshake at someone?"

"Only if they support fascism. We consider it an opening salvo," Penny said. Her father was in the military and studied World War 2 history. She had heard this sort of language all the time while growing up. But although the word had no tangible meaning to the other girls, they got the idea behind it anyways. The firm and resolved manner used in delivery was enough to convey its purpose: Penny meant business and her confidence appealed to them.

"Well, she might get expelled," Hannah said snottily.

"We must go to her aid, then," Penny proclaimed. "That is, unless you feel it is a bad look to do so."

"Oh, we were going to show up no matter what," Alyssa said.

Penny scanned the group of girls. After a cursory analysis she noticed one of them seemed a bit shy and possibly impressionable.

"What's your name?" she asked in a tone that compelled an answer.

"Me? I'm… My name is Mandy," she replied.

Mandy had just recently come out as a lesbian and was in that period in which she was fully embraced by all of the other females around her. Hannah was particularly interested to be seen as protective of her. She had even said once right after she found out Mandy was gay: "If I wasn't straight I'd totally beaver-dam you."

"I'm Penny," the tall, slender, steely-eyed girl said. "Mandy, I hope G can count on you."

The girl blushed and nodded in a shy way that showed how easily a few words of confidence could disarm her.

"Uh, yes, you can count on me," Mandy said softly.

Hannah had had enough. She stepped between Penny and the rest of the girls, particularly using her butt to block G's mouthpiece from making further advances.

"Hey, we should really go show G some support."

Penny didn't budge. She wasn't going to allow Hannah the satisfaction. She crossed her arms and waited to make eye contact with the redhead when she turned back around.

"That's a good idea," Penny said while locking her gaze on the sorority sister's green eyes.

Hannah paused to consider. She wasn't expecting that.

"G's hearing is tomorrow at the Student Union conference room," Penny said, wrestling control of the conversation back "10am."

This was the first time the girls were detached from looking down at their phones. With their heads up right they waited for marching orders. A silence hung in the air for a brief moment. No clicking, no swiping, no self-satisfied laughter--- It was all about perception.

"We'll be there!" Mandy called out suddenly.

Penny nodded.

"Good."

Chapter 4

Tyler headed back to the freshman dorm. It was still segregated by floor: girls on the first, guys on the second. There were a few hook ups, but mostly the girls stayed on the bottom floor. Tyler spotted Rosanna, a tattooed gamer girl he was crushing on. She was folding her clothes in the laundry room near the lobby when Tyler walked by.

"Rosanna, 'sup? Missed you in class," said Tyler, trying to be in cool guy mode as much as possible. "League of Legends later?"

"Yeah, maybe," she said noncommittal.

Tyler continued up the stairs, unsure if he should pursue the conversion. He frowned when he reached the second floor. Maybe he should just ask her out or would it be weird dating someone living in the same building?

"What's up, fuck nuts?" greeted Tyler, dropping onto the couch in the second floor lounge of the New Building. "Ow! What's this couch made of? Bags of sand?"

"You can't flop down on that, bro," answered Greg Merril, who was texting on his phone. "Dorm furniture's not your parents' living room. How was that thing?"

Tyler got out his sketch book and started sketching with a charcoal pencil as he answered. He was drawing G as an angry milkshake.

"Crazy. Some lesbian tossed a milkshake at the speaker," said Tyler. "Her and the rest of the LGBTQ, ABC or whatever--- disrupted the whole thing."

"You shouldn't say that," Kyle North, Greg's roommate said.

"Shut the Hell up, Kyle," said Greg, already sick of him.

"It's just problematic, is what I'm saying," Kyle weakly defended.

"You're gonna have a problematic if you fuckin' correct me again," Greg threatened.

"Shouldn't you be somewhere following Heather instructions?" teased Tyler. "You pussy whipped motherfucker."

"Screw you," Kyle bristled.

Derrick Dromond, Tyler's roommate, rushed to the lounge and leaned in holding both sides of the doorway.

"C'mon, dude, we going to this thing?" he asked anxiously.

"Derrick, it's over," Tyler informed him. "I told you it was at seven."

"Dammit!" he said "I thought you said eight."

"Bro, it's 8:45 now," laughed Greg.

"Well, great," he sighed, sitting in the chair nearby. "You tell me what happened. I gotta talk about it in Poly-Sci with Professor Mumbles."

"You got Franklin?" asked Tyler.

"Yeah, why? Who'd you get?"

"Mondel. He's cool. Switch over. Some of the girls dropped out."

"Nah. Mumbles feels like a guy I can intimidate a full letter grade," Derrick theorized. "Mondel sounds like he would make me work."

"He'd talk about your Libertarian shit all day long," assured Tyler.

"Don't call it shit," Derrick said. "It's a way of life."

"Not if you want to get laid," Greg assured him. "You start talking about that free speech and liberty--- The vaginas go dry."

"It's not about getting laid," Derrick countered.

"It's **always** about getting laid, bro," Greg assured him, continuing to type. "If you ain't woke, you ain't seein' titties. Check this out."

Greg started to read his text aloud in a whiny, breathless voice.

"'People of color are getting a raw deal these days. I know that I come from a background of white privilege, but I hope you and I can get past it and come to a more woke understanding.'" read Greg.

"Does that shit work?" asked Tyler, incredulous.

Greg's phone buzzed. He read the reply and stood up immediately.

"I'm meeting her for a latte in twenty. You tell me," Greg announced, showing off his phone's reply screen. "If you'll excuse me, gents. I have to powder my balls."

"Oh, no," muttered Kyle as his roommate left. "Can I—"

"No," Tyler said immediately. "You can't sleep in our room just because your roomie's having sex. You snore."

"Yeah, just sleep in here," Derrick said, gesturing to the room. "Who's gonna bother you?"

"I might," quipped a voice.

Turning toward the noise, the group noticed Billy Sighn. Billy was a small Indian kid that had scrunched up his feet behind the dorm's weird, mid-

28

room couch divider. With the lights half off and TV not on, no one had noticed him.

"Shit, Billy, what the fuck?" laughed a startled Tyler. "You spyin' on us?"

"I like to listen," he admitted. "Your dynamic fascinates me. Plus I am in the middle of writing a paper. Chenk has our room filled with the pot smoke."

"As a Libertarian, I support him getting high, but that guy takes it too far," said Derrick.

"Is Chenk trying to see how much THC the human body can withstand or something?" joked Tyler.

"I don't know," said Billy. "I think his life is just sad and he wishes to forget. Perhaps we should take him to the movies or something. Get him out of the dorm."

"Fuck movies," dismissed Tyler. "Who goes to movies anymore?"

"Who reads comic books anymore?" quipped Billy.

"Yeah, ever since Marvel got woke--- Movies are total shit now," Derrick said. "I can't watch a flick unless there's some hot chick doing hot chick stuff."

"Titties mandatory?" asked Tyler, putting bigger boobs on the milkshake.

"I wouldn't say no to fun bags," Derrick qualified. "Certainly if there is bush and titties, that's a major factor."

"There should be a sex scene," added Billy.

"Yeah!"

"Guys, you're talking about porn," Tyler said.

"No, not porn. Porn is porn!" Derrick explained. "You gotta have a little romance, a little sex---"

"Like Game of Thrones?" asked Tyler.

"Too much dudity," dismissed Derrick, sitting up and now on track. "I can't see a movie without titties, a smoking hot babe, who has at least one sex scene and no naked guy parts. I don't even want to see his ass."

"Yeah," agreed Tyler, wrinkling his brow.

"Right? I mean, who wants to see that?" asked Derrick.

"Girls?" offered Billy.

"They don't want to see that," assured Derrick.

Kyle suddenly shut his laptop noisily and headed back to his room.

"God, that guy's a pussy," said Tyler.

"No butts for the women? They don't like that?" asked Billy, trying to understand.

"No," assured Derrick. "Men are visual. We seek out fertile physical traits. Wide hips, symmetrical face, big titties--- Evolutionary speaking, we trying to find mates to impregnate."

"This is science, so okay," agreed Billy.

"Women evolved on a different track," Derrick said. "They are looking for providers."

"But big strong men," countered Billy.

"Yeah, but it's more than that. Classically, a big strong guy in Neolithic times--- Can't go wrong, right? But even in that era, if you're stupid and can't hunt--- It didn't matter. For them, it's about providing for the spawn. Security. Money. A good job," Derrick preached.

"Then why do all the girls end up with Greg?" asked Billy.

"Dude, because that guy's a manwhore," Tyler joked. "He's providing cock!"

"It's the free market of vagina," corrected Derrick. "College coeds are still going with the easiest, big-guy traits. They don't know what they want. Once they figure out stuff like that, then you and me--- We're in."

"What about me?" Tyler objected.

"Dude, you're a cartoonist," Derrick said in disappointment. "You're gonna be broke. But you can get laid before the chicks figure that out. I mean, they have to disappoint their fathers with somebody."

Tyler showed the guys his finished piece. It was a very angry milkshake with massive tits, attacking like a commando.

"Don't show them that," Derrick laughed.

Chapter 5

Mondel was living in a student apartment on the edge of town. It was a high-end, spacious place designed for four. This left him plenty of room to have Zoe on his weekends and the ability to bank money. He was saving for a new house, the old one having been sold in the divorce.

He didn't wake up the next morning because he never really got any sleep. Sometime around six he just gave up and got out of bed. Now instead of thinking about saving up for a house, he was wondering how long his savings would last if he got fired over this.

Did he say or do anything that might've been captured on video? Would it be taken out of context? He had tenure, but what was that worth these days? The professor would protect him, but realistically, if Albert threw him under the bus what could he do? Sue the college while trying to juggle alimony payments and child support **and** look for a new job?

After three quarters of a pot of coffee and a bagel with cream cheese, he headed up to hill for the department meeting. Professor P said it was mandatory and almost nothing he did was mandatory in the entire time he worked under him.

Arriving early to the faculty conference room, he found that the rest of department had already beaten him to the table. Fawkes, Martinez, Franklin and Papadopoulos. The air was tinged with anxiety.

"Shut the door, please Lawrence," requested Papadopoulos.

Mondel did as he said and sat down. There was an awkward moment of silence.

"All right," sighed P. "Tell us what happened."

"Greizer set up, starting giving his talk. A few minutes in, I heard some students trying to get into Cicero Hall through the doors on stage right. Then one of the students in the audience opened them. This G came in with a group of girls," Mondel told.

"G? As in…"

"I think it stands for Gina. The one that dropped out of my class along with Penny," Mondel clarified.

"What did the girls do?" asked Fawkes.

"They didn't waste any time. They started chanting and disrupting the talk," Mondel explained. "Greizer tried to engage with them, but they called him a fascist and a supporter of misogyny and racism."

"Is he?" asked Fawkes.

"No!" snapped Professor P. "Do you think Lawrence would invite a speaker like that to campus?"

"Was he on Fox News?" asked Fawkes.

"He's promoting a book. They all go on there," Diana dismissed. "Besides, his book was about Political Centrism."

"Oh," said Franklin, understanding.

"The mummy speaks," noted the professor.

"What?" asked Mondel.

"C'mon, mummy, finish your thought," prompted the prof.

"Centrists are just the worst kind of people," stated Franklin matter-of-factly. "The Press of New York had a fascinating article citing the International Values Survey of 2011 to 2015 and the American Values Survey of 2009. It was in an opinion piece by Dr. Joshua Steinberg."

"Sounds like he already cherry picked his conclusion, but continue," prompted P.

"Well, it seems that Centrists are more likely to support authoritarian governments," Franklin explained. "Anyone that supports the status quo in this day and age, truly isn't thinking clearly. Obviously the students are reacting to the rise in misogyny and racism in our institutions."

"You're talking like you're not **part** of the institution," Mondel said. "And you understand, Greizer is African-American."

"Does that matter?" Franklin questioned.

"When you call a guy a racist in public?" said the professor sarcastically. "Yeah, I think it matters."

"Did you try and engage the students?" asked Diana, attempting to steer the conversation away from Franklin.

"Yes, but they were totally unreasonable. They wouldn't acknowledge the most basic of facts," Mondel said frustratingly. "It's like objective reality meant nothing."

"Well, facts are relative," Franklin added. "Foucault says---"

"Mel, stop bringing up fucking Foucault," the professor said, shutting him down. "Seriously, this is not helping."

"I don't see the problem here," Fawkes added. "The students have the right to protest fascism."

"The speaker **wasn't** a fascist," snapped Mondel.

"Well, they perceived him as such," countered Fawkes.

"Which is relative to their perspective," pointed out Franklin.

"Yeah, which doesn't mean a single flying fuck," growled Papadopoulos. "**We're** the adults on this campus and they are the children! Even if Foucault was right, do you want freshmen girls straight out of high school deciding what is and isn't right for the college you short-sighted halfwit?!"

"You don't have to insult me," Franklin blushed, backing off.

"Sorry, it's just what I saw from my **relative** position," the prof said sarcastically.

"We should be proud of these students," Fawkes insisted. "They applied Rules for Radicals in the second semester! They're very advanced."

"You assigned first semester **freshmen** students to read **Alinsky**?!" Professor P said outraged.

"Yes!" Fawkes said proudly. "Why? Is that bad?"

"They haven't even completed Poly-Sci 101! What the fuck do they know to protest or be radical about Fawkes? Not getting enough likes on Instagram?!" snapped P. "I should have your fucking job, Fawkes! You're not fit to grade Kindergartens at a fucking **grammar** school, you irresponsible Commie-tard!"

"Sir, that is uncalled for," protested Fawkes. "I should---"

"You should what? You should what?" P said, getting into his face. "You wanna go over my head to Albert? Be my guest! You tell him about this PR clusterfuck and see what you get! Tell him you're partially responsible for it! Because as far as you're concerned, you're **totally** responsible for it, you brainless Trotskyite!"

The room became unbearably silent for a few moments. Mondel continued.

"Anyhow, Greizer struggled through the rest of the presentation with the girls chanting," explained Mondel. "Just before I could get him out of the room, G hit him with the milkshake. Ruined a very expensive suit. He was not happy."

"Why didn't Safety and Security do something?" asked Martinez.

"They had come, but they went outside to consult their supervisor," Mondel explained. "Once the milkshake hit, they finally arrested her."

"You think Grezier is likely to sue?" asked P.

"No, as long as we pay for his suit and the books that got ruined, I think he'll be okay with that," Mondel surmised.

"See? No harm, no foul," added Fawkes.

"She assaulted him," Diana pointed out.

"With a milkshake," laughed Fawkes. "It's a trend."

"Fawkes, would you like me to **trend** you with this hot cup of coffee?" threatened Papadopoulos. "Would that be nice and **trendy** for you?"

"Oh, sure," said Fawkes. "When a white male does something, it's 'boys will be boys', but when women of color do it---"

"**I'm** a woman of color," Diana pointed out. "I think she **assaulted** him. What does that make me?"

"Kind of an Uncle Tom," said Fawkes.

"You piece of shit!" growled Diana, grabbing her coffee cup.

"Diana," said the professor, staying her hand. "Fawkes, you say another word in this meeting and I swear to **Christ** I will make sure you spend the rest of your miserable Commie life as an adjunct grading papers in the fucking basement."

Professor P waited. For a second, it looked like Fawkes might say something, but thought better of it.

"Okay, here's what we're going to do," Papadopoulos announced. "Since Greizer seems fine, it just remains for us to discipline the girl so this doesn't happen again. We'll take the heat off the department by dropping it into the lap of the student government."

"I don't know, prof," said Mondel warily. "The kids seem pretty mad."

"Exactly," acknowledged the professor. "The student government will give her some slap on the wrist and then the whole thing will be over. You'll have to appear, of course."

"Me?" objected Mondel. "It's a student government."

"Yes, but you're a witness and they're going to have some inquiry," the professor said. "Just sit there and pretend the college kids are doing something important. Then just agree with their punishment and this will all be over. Compliment them on how mature they're all acting, teachable moment, blah, blah, blah--- And it's done."

"Sure," Mondel forced himself to agree.

"No one's blaming you, Lawrence," the professor assured. "Certainly having campus speakers has been part of the college experience for decades."

Fawkes threw up his hands, outraged he couldn't protest. Professor P glared at him, hoping he would say something. Fawkes folded his arms and looked away.

Chapter 6

After his Intro to Comparative Politics class, Mondel had a lunch date with Celia. The theater professor had been on him for a few days about visiting the Vegan V. It was a café on the Commons that one of Celia's old students ran.

Normally, Mondel would've been fretting about the meet for days. But with everything happening and suddenly being so intense in his department, he was distracted enough just to show up without over thinking it.

"Hey," she greeted.

"Hey," smiled Mondel, relieved to be away from the stress for now.

Celia was a thin, fit hippie 40-something with brown hair in braids and long slender hands. She wore leggings, boots and a jacket over a flowery top. She smelled a little like Patchouli oil and incense. Mondel pictured her doing a lot of yoga in her free time.

"You seemed stressed," she sensed.

"Rough day at the office," he smirked.

"I heard. Some of my students were talking."

"Hi! Welcome to Vegan V! I'm Nina!" said the perky waitress, also a student. "Have you guys been here before? Do you know what you want?"

Nina had inserted herself into the conversation in a rather jarring manner. Mondel and Celia scrambled to look at the menu.

"Oh, I'll be right back with water. You want water, right?" she checked.

"Sure," Mondel said, putting down the menu.

The waitress toddled off to the kitchen.

"Anyhow, what did your class say about it?" the doctor asked, hoping to feel the pulse of the student body.

"They didn't articulate it well, but something about a Trump supporter coming to campus?" she half-recalled. "He was yelling homophobic slurs at people?"

"That is not what happened at all," insisted Mondel.

Nina came rushing back, spilling some of the water across his place setting.

"Oh, sorry," she said, sounding like she was in a hurry. "Did you decide?"

"I'd like the Portobello sandwich on gluten-free, multigrain bread," ordered Celia.

Mondel tried to skim the menu quickly. He felt rushed by the waitress and the font on the menu made the whole enterprise confusing. The typeface was from a computer, but looked handwritten and was barely readable.

"Do you have a large salad with like, chicken or something?" he asked.

"No chicken. It's vegan," she shrugged.

"Bring me a large salad then, with vinaigrette," he requested. "And an iced tea."

"'Kay," she responded.

Nina walked away without taking the menus. Mondel sighed, picked them up and put them on the next table over.

"Your students actually believe that happened?" he asked. "You know that didn't happen, right?"

"I assumed they were being hyperbolic, especially when they described the Klansmen bodyguards," she said, amused.

"The speaker was African-American," Mondel corrected.

"Kind of weird he supports Trump then," she noted.

"He didn't---"

Mondel stopped himself from snapping. He couldn't believe the rumor had gotten so out of hand, so fast.

"He didn't support Trump. He wrote a book on Political Centrism," explained the doctor.

"Well, he must've said something triggering," Celia assumed.

"He never got a chance to say much of anything," Mondel explained. "The students just charged in the room and started yelling at him. Then, after disrupting the entire talk, they hit him with a milkshake."

"Oh, jeez," she laughed. "That sounds like something I'd do back then. Remember those days?"

"Well, sure, but I didn't throw milkshakes at speakers. Did you?"

"Let's see, I protested abortion restrictions and flashed my tits. They said 'Restrict this!' across them," she recounted. "I marched for gay rights, I

36

marched against nuclear power and I know I protested a war over something. Or was it Women's Rights? So long ago!"

"Yeah, but you protested, you didn't assault anyone," pointed out Mondel.

"It's a milkshake, Lawrence," she laughed.

"He could still sue the college. It could've been filled with rocks or some kind of bleach--- He didn't know," Mondel speculated. "But more importantly, this guy didn't deserve that. He wasn't some kind of extremist. It's like the Overton Window has moved too far."

"Overton Window, what is that?" she asked, having recalled reading or hearing about it once.

"If you graph political opinion, the window is the part of the graph on the inside, right?" Mondel explained, drawing on a napkin. "So normally the window looks like this."

Mondel drew a box, a line down the middle and put a curve that was split more or less equally.

"The line in the middle is where most people are. The curve charts political opinion from, let's say just five years ago," explained the doctor. "This is a typical Overton Window, but now…"

Redrawing the illustration, Mondel moved the line to the left.

"The further extremists on the left drag the window farther and farther, the more it puts everyone on the right," he explained. "Now Left-Centrists are right wing, normal Republicans are now far right and Conservatives alt-right or extreme."

"Well, that does sound kind of correct," Celia said gingerly. "Not that I call every Republican a Nazi, but…"

"Look, I'm a Liberal. Always have been," Mondel said. "I voted Clinton and Obama, but I want our side to win on ideas. You can't win over people by throwing milkshakes at them."

"I guess I see your point," she conceded. "What's the college going to do?"

"Fortunately, the speaker isn't going to press charges," Mondel sighed. "We're going to let the student government dole out the punishment."

"Oh, God," she laughed. "Are you serious?"

"Why, what's wrong with that?"

"Have you been to a student government meeting?" she guffawed, coughing a bit. "Oh, God. Sorry."

"You've been?"

"Yeah, we have to get our money for the plays we put on from them," she explained. "It's mostly a formality. If they actually denied us, we could just go over their heads, but we still go through the motions every year."

"Are they...competent?"

"About as competent as our waitress," she muttered, as Nina returned.

Nina placed their orders in front of the two professors. She dropped the bowl of salad so hard, some of the leaves popped out. Rather than correct her, they waited until she went back into the kitchen to switch plates.

"Wow, this is kind of a small salad," said Mondel, poking around with his fork. "I'm wondering how much this is going to cost me."

Mondel attempted to peek inside the menu, but he didn't see prices.

"There aren't prices," explained Celia. "This is a pay-what-you-want place. This is on me though. You don't ever want to get the check here."

"Why would I pay anything then? I guess because I feel sorry for her?" asked Mondel, confused.

"Yeah, but when you do pay, there's also an 18% man tax," she explained. "This place is run by one of my former students, she's...trying."

Chapter 7

After lunch, Mondel walked Celia back to her car. He debated on whether or not to take her hand. They cut through the Commons and he smiled remembering his college days.

"What?" asked Celia, noticing the smile.

"Just remembering," he replied.

"Oh, right, you went to school here," she recalled. "Has it changed much? The town?"

"Not really," he said scrunching up his nose trying to think of the right phrase to describe his nostalgia. "It's like what Karr said about change. Except for the students, maybe."

"Not on my campus," Celia chuckled. "But San Francisco has always been different."

"Why didn't you stay there?" asked Mondel, hoping to learn something new about her.

"I don't know," she dithered. "Had to make my own way. Spread the joy or something. Plus I couldn't afford to live there on a professor's salary."

As they passed by the shops on the Commons, Mondel noticed Upstate Comics. The store had been there since before he was a student and he'd frequent it on occasion with his friends. They were having a going-out-of-business sale.

"Oh, no," said Mondel, disappointed. "The comic store is closing."

"Did you read comics? I never did," Celia said. "Another one bites the dust, huh?"

"I want to do a quick browse," said Mondel.

"You go ahead, I should get back to campus," she said a little too anxiously. "Call me...or text me. 'Kay?"

"Yeah," said Mondel, annoyed with himself that he hadn't taken her hand.

Was Celia not into him? Was that a kissing moment lost? She was so casual about their encounter, it seemed like pressing the issue would've been weird. Too heavy for the moment. Mondel made a mental note to set up the next date somewhere more romantic. He needed to send out a signal that he wanted something more physical.

Walking into Upstate Comics, he was immediately struck by the smell. It was a combination of paper, dust, microwaved cheese and B.O. The store hadn't changed. It was still covered in posters of all his favorite superheroes and had rows of white boxes with comics. Everything was 40, 60, 80 percent off, depending.

The guy behind the counter, Clark, had seen better days. Mondel remembered him from the 90's when he was an energetic comic book store owner that talked knowledgeably about price, condition and storyline. Clark's hair had receded with just enough in the back to still make a ponytail. He used to wear neatly pressed polo shirts with the Upstate Comics logo. He was sitting at the counter, gut hanging over a Wolverine t-shirt, eating ramen from a bowl.

"Hey," he said, half-heartedly.

"Hey," Mondel greeted, looking around the store.

And that was about the extent of Clark's customer service skills. He sort of vaguely remembered Mondel, but then again--- He sort of vaguely remembered everyone that used to come into his store.

Mondel scanned the racks. The wash of color looked unfamiliar and confusing. Had they changed all the characters since he had stopped buying?

"Sorry to see you're going out of business," Mondel said. "I used to shop here when I was a student."

"Yeah, so did a lot of people," sighed Clark. "What happened to you?"

"Oh, I uh---" stammered Mondel, not ready for such a direct inquiry. "Had a kid, got a job--- Guess I just didn't have time for this anymore."

Mondel noticed the Wolverine on his t-shirt actually had boobs and was a woman.

"Is Wolverine a woman now?" he asked.

"Yeah," replied Clark, sounding tired of explaining it. "A lot of characters are now. Your son read comics?"

"Daughter, actually," he corrected.

Clark suddenly perked up a little.

"Oh, well, then I have plenty of titles she'd like. Spider-Fem, The Amazing Marsupial Girl, The Vagilanties and the new---"

"Actually," interrupted Mondel. "She's never read a comic or expressed an interest. I was just thinking for me as an old Dark Knight fan."

"Oh," said Clark, deflating and going back down into his chair. "All that stuff is gone."

"Gone?" repeated Mondel in disbelief. "That was--- I mean, that was the whole thing. Superheroes."

"First there was Gamergate and then there was Comicsgate," Clark stated as if he was rattling off a list of political scandals. "Everything's toxic masculinity now. If your comic or video game isn't appropriately diverse…"

He trailed off gesturing he was tired of the whole thing. He was getting out while he could. This way he could recoup some money.

"The students used to be like you," he remembered. "They'd come down from the hill and buy a few issues. They actually read them. Now all they do is come in here to complain. I don't make the damned comics! I just try and sell them!"

Mondel felt bad for the guy. Clark seemed frustrated and broken, like one of those autoworkers whose job had been sent overseas. He grabbed a few issues off the rack and purchased them. He wanted to get out of the sad depressing store that now reeked of death.

Walking back to his car, Mondel flipped through the comics. The artwork that once jumped off the page with thrilling images that inspired him were now staid and still born. Every panel felt like clip art compiled by a corporate drone who was looking to complete his or her job as quickly as possible. The dialogue was painful and preachy. Characters that once saved the world and literally moved mountains, now couldn't get it together to "do adulting right". They bristled under the idea of responsibility, unless it was to even a score regarding a perceived sleight. Most of all, he noticed, the characters didn't do much of anything. They reminded him of his students…

Because they did sit around and complain.

At the edge of the parking lot, Mondel dumped them in the trash. He didn't just not want to read them, at that moment, he wanted to make sure no one read them. He shoved them down past the lip of the trash can to make sure no kid might fish them out and try to look at them later.

Chapter 8

For a day or two, it seemed like things would die down on campus. Yes, rumors were swirling about what happened, but distractions on the Internet were quickly drawing away the students' attention. At least, it felt that way when the student government organized their meeting. Mondel was almost calm when he arrived at the Student Union conference room.

"Dr. Mondel? I'm Chance Williams, Student Government President," introduced the smartly dressed junior sitting in a wheelchair. "Thank you for taking time for us today."

Chance was an older student. He had gone to Upstate on a GI bill after being paralyzed by an IED in Afghanistan. Mondel instantly liked him and could see he had that young politician look about him. He would probably run for office one day and Mondel could see himself voting for him.

"Have you been briefed on what's going to happen?" asked Mondel.

"No, but I think I know the lay of the land here," Chance said knowingly. "You guys didn't want to slap down one of the gay students publicly, so you're making us do it."

Mondel sidestepped the question.

"The college can't let something like this go unpunished, but we're not interested in crucifying her," Mondel explained. "We'd all just like this to be over."

"I read ya, doc," Chance said, understanding. "Back in Afghanistan, when things went fubar, we had a process too. I get it."

The doctor exhaled and finally relaxed. Here was an actual adult who understood the real world. This would all be over soon.

The student government set up in the conference room. Chance was in the center. Also in attendance was a stenographer taking minutes, the treasurer, the vice president and the parliamentarian. Mondel sat on the opposite side but

42

far down on one end near the treasurer, Laney Wang. Several chairs were set up across from the table for G and presumably some of her friends.

"Would you like some water, Dr. Mondel?" asked Laney.

"Thanks, great," Mondel accepted.

Laney poured him water into a plastic cup. The government took care of some business. They were mostly in charge of the money for campus clubs and events. The biggest decision they had to make was which band was going to play on campus or which comedians might visit, not that the latter did anymore. It was rare that they had to throw their weight behind anything like this, but Chance took the process seriously.

As Mondel set his cup on the table, a low rumble started to permeate the outside of the building. It was as if something large and ominous were approaching. Mondel noted that the water in his cup was starting to vibrate as the sound of the mob grew near. Then the door burst open and chaos entered.

"Two-four-six-eight! We don't want your fascist hate! Two-four-six-eight! We don't want your fascist hate!"

G, Penny and a coterie of angry protesters, mostly girls, had arrived. Trailing in behind and filling up the ranks were black clad boys with bandanas on their faces. They carried Antifa flags and wore gloves. Several of the girls were videotaping everything on their phones.

"Hey-hey-hey!" shouted Chance. "Turn it down! Now!"

"You don't get to tell us what to do, cis male!" shouted one of the girls from the back.

The angry mob agreed.

"Look, we're just having a hearing on this," explained Chance. "This isn't a trial, but we're supposed to dole out some kind of discipline. Are you trying to make it worse?"

G took a seat and the other protesters seemed to follow her lead. They either sat or calmed down for the moment. With the crowd momentarily under control, Chance called the minutes of the meeting and wasted no time getting into it.

"All right, obviously you're passionate about your beliefs," he acknowledged. "I respect that. Tell us about what happened."

"G, was defending herself from---" began Penny.

"Excuse me," interrupted Chance. "I'd like to hear from the accused."

Mondel liked this. Chance had actually managed to correct Penny and get the upper hand in the conversation. Penny backed down and G leaned forward to speak. She'd have to admit some kind of culpability in this mess and it would be over.

43

"I don't recognize the authority of a white male oppressor over me," G announced. "You have no right to judge me."

The mob cheered wildly.

"I'm the student government president," Chance reminded her. "I have the authority based on a vote that you participated in."

"I didn't vote for you," explained G. "Voting is strictly patriarchal."

"I'm the treasurer," Laney pointed out.

"Okay, well, did you throw the milkshake or not?" asked Chance, trying to move things along.

"I defended myself from an attack by fascist forces that attempt to further marginalize people like me!" G said, building in fiery rhetoric. "Bringing this speaker to campus was an attack on all of us! His words were violence."

"Well, I've actually been to Afghanistan where I've seen **actual** violence," trolled Chance. "So I wouldn't call what the speaker did **that**."

"How do you know? You weren't there!" accused Penny.

"And that's why Dr. Mondel's here," gestured Chance to Mondel.

Mondel felt his whole body go tense. Never had he been so anxious and afraid with students looking at him. The mob made low level booing noises.

"Doc, please tell us as a witness, what happened that night," requested Chance, feeling like he was checkmating the opposition.

"Ahem," began Mondel nervously. "On the night in question, we had a speaker, a Mr. Grezier---"

"Fascist!" yelled one of the students.

"He wasn't a fascist," Mondel countered, tired of saying it. "He wrote a book on Political **Centrism**."

"Same as a Nazi!" added one of the Antifa members.

"Dr. Mondel, you're a doctor of political science, are you not?" asked Chance.

"That's correct."

"And as such, you know the difference between Nazis, fascists and political centrists, right?"

"That I do."

"Are political centrists Nazis or fascists?" asked Chance.

"No."

The mob booed him.

"That's just your opinion!" shouted Penny, outraged.

"I have a **doctorate** in Political Science," Mondel repeated incredulous.

"Yeah," scoffed G. "From other fascist **white** men."

44

The mob seemed to agree with that assessment, completely devaluing Mondel's expertise.

"This is insane," Mondel scoffed.

"That's a microaggression against the differently-abled!" accused Penny. "Totally problematic!"

"Stop correcting language, please!" snapped Mondel. "You want to know what Fascism is? That's Fascism!"

"If you want to keep making those mistakes, 'doctor'," G dismissed. "You keep living in the 1970's."

"The 1970's was **progressive!**" insisted Mondel. "And I'm only 45!"

"The witness will continue," ordered Chance, trying to make things happen.

"G and her friends disrupted the entire talk for an hour and when Greizer was leaving--- That's when G threw the milkshake," said Mondel.

"And you saw the milkshake thrown and hit the speaker?" asked Chance.

"Yes, then Safety and Security arrested her," Mondel added.

"All right," said Chance wrapping things up. "While the student government supports your right to free speech, we cannot condone assault on campus. I hereby order you to do 48 hours of community service to be served at your convenience this school year."

The mob erupted angrily. They were not having it.

"This man is lying!" insisted Penny, pointing at Mondel. "He is a Nazi!"

"I'm Jewish!" Mondel objected, pointing to himself.

"You're part of the same white male dominated culture!" insisted Penny. "You saw what your white male eyes wanted you to see! Not the truth!"

"This entire student government is a white cis power structure," dismissed G, to the cheers of the mob.

"Hello! I'm an Asian woman," objected Laney.

"And I'm a disabled vet!" Chance added.

Penny and G continued to rant, oblivious to the facts and people around them.

"You're just trying to marginalize people of color to build upon your own white power!" Penny continued. "This racist institution must end! White power has to end! When do the marginalized people get to speak?!"

"**You're** white!" pointed out Laney.

"We do not recognize the authority of this student government!" G proclaimed. "We're calling for a new government! We're taking our fight to the people and the streets!"

The mob cheered wildly. So confident in their victory, G and Penny stood up chanting and marched out of the hearing.

"Streets?" thought Mondel.

"Two, four, six eight! We don't want your fascist hate! Two-four-six-eight! We don't want your fascist hate!"

Chapter 9

The LGBTQIA+ Alliance held an emergency meeting at Baker Hall between Whitcock Hall and the Theater Building. Baker Hall had several ballrooms that were used for student dances and other functions back when those were still a thing. By this point it had become a place for various groups to gather, including RPGers, LARPers, cosplayers, trivia game geeks, cinephiles, and various other factions of fringe student life.

Meetings were organized on various internet sites and apps, namely Twitter, Reddit, Discord, among others. Sites like Facebook had fallen out of favor in recent years, as the students said too many old people were on there. They felt it had become a place where only wedding announcements, vacation photos, funeral notices, and baby pictures were posted. It was far removed from their reality. That kind of life, the quote unquote normal one, might never be theirs, or if was on the horizon, they wanted to stave it off for as long as possible.

Charlene Kannel was the leader of the Alliance. She was a grad student who had been enrolled at Upstate longer than anyone else. She was practically an academic careerist. If she had her way she'd stay in class forever.

She took over the Alliance after her mentor, Karen Francis, got her PhD and became the chair of the Gender Studies department. She was a proponent of Third Wave Feminism and was just starting to understand and incorporate Fourth Wave ideas into her classes.

Charlene sat behind an 8-foot fold-out table with a Rainbow Pride Flag, complete with the name LGBTQIA+ Alliance on it, draped in front. She looked over the group of concerned students sitting in rows of fold-out chairs. She counted many friendly faces, including her lesbian sisters, gay allies, and a couple of trans athletes who were breaking women's records left and right. Some in the group were genderqueer, meaning they neither identified as female

47

or male, but as non-binary. She didn't understand it, but she was working to accept it.

All-in-all Charlene was a reasonable woman. She held supportive, productive, informative, and oftentimes entertaining meetings. She could tell a joke and take one too. There was a balance to her.

"Thanks for showing up," she said to the room. "I know we want to talk about the milkshake incident and what's going on with all the attention the college is getting, but are there any other items we should discuss first?"

A genderqueer person with short buzzed hair, pierced nose, and a denim jacket with a white tank-top underneath stood up.

"They haven't changed the signs on the bathrooms yet to reflect all genders. You hear about when that's happening?"

"Last I heard they were waiting on the signs. Pretty sure any delay is on the manufacturer, not the College," Charlene answered.

"Ok, cool," the person said and sat down.

"Oh, I did want to bring up the spring sports schedule," Charlene said. "I know we have several trans athletes competing on women's teams and events. There was some protest last semester but we were told by the Athletic Department those records will stand. I'm sure they'll contact you directly as well but they wanted it heard by everyone in the Alliance first."

The trans athletes looked pleased. Charlene felt a bit of resignation, but before she could say anything G and Penny entered the room. G limped along with her cane, flanked by several members of Antifa. Penny circled around from front to back to get a gauge of who was in attendance.

After a grand entrance G stopped about fifteen feet from Charlene. Penny walked up and stood by her side.

"G demands to be heard," Penny stated with authority.

"We were just going to talk about the hearing. Was she vindicated?" Charlene asked.

"G does not need to be vindicated. Just by existing she is validated," Penny responded.

"Well, we have some students here who have concerns to voice. If G can be patient she will have her turn to speak," Charlene explained.

"She? What makes you assume G is female?" Penny replied. "Assumptions are usually a sign of privilege. We all know since gay marriage equality was achieved lesbians and gays have enjoyed an uptick in parity with those who are straight, cisnormative and part of the establishment."

"Look, I'm happy to call G whatever G wants to be called," Charlene answered carefully.

Penny was indeed planting a minefield. Charlene wondered how best to tip-toe to avoid them, or should she just run forward and set them all off at once. She wished she could consult Karen, who in her mind had better debate skills, but knew this was her time to lead.

"I am They," G said while stepping forward two feet. "Not he, not she. Something else."

"I'm well aware of non-binary identification," Charlene said.

"Not non-binary," G said with a tone of revelatory inflection. "Rather, They is **post**-binary."

Charlene was confused. She looked around the members of the Alliance, but could no longer find a friendly face amongst them to connect with. G's words were resonating.

"If everything is indeed subjective, then They is not beholden to any power other than what They generate themselves."

"That sort of pseudo intellectual inspired circular logic doesn't hold any currency here," Charlene pushed back. She knew she had to show some force to keep this from getting out of hand. It's what Karen would do.

"Ah, currency, another construct keeping the systems of the current powers in place. We will no longer have a need for fiat chains once The Post-Binary Collective dissolves society's self-imposed constraints."

No one spoke for a few moments. The Antifa members, with their black scarves covering the faces, scanned the room for any sign of trouble. But all they saw were students who weren't exactly sure who was in charge right now.

Charlene was about to say something when G moved forward two more steps, with more purpose and conviction.

"I was found guilty by their government, but I do not accept their verdict," G proclaimed. "They cannot tell Them what to say, how to act, what to do. So they must be unseated.

"For far too long we have bowed to them. The constant struggle between oppressed and oppressor. For us, no more. No more, I say! We must break from the madness and build a new world.

"Can I count on those who want to be a part of this new world, this new Collective? Can I call upon **The**?"

Charlene had had enough. She stood up and came from behind the table. Her big frame carried what seemed like the body of a linebacker. Her black Indigo Girls t-shirt was faded, probably bought at a concert back when G was just a toddler. And now she had to stand face-to-face with that former toddler who was now a person barely of legal age to vote.

"This meeting was called to help everyone deal with the aftermath of your milkshake incident," Charlene said. "The media is descending on us and frankly we don't want the attention."

"Why would you?" G asked rhetorically. "You already have what you want. But The Collective appreciates your efforts, all you have done for the cause..."

There was a pause. A strange coyness emerged from within G, but it lasted just for a brief moment. Just long enough for her to say...

"Although you did forsake us after Stonewall."

"I wasn't at Stonewall," Charlene stated plainly.

"Oh, but you carry it with you," G said. "Your sacred day. There were genderqueer and trans people there as well, but they didn't look good in your history books or at your events. But I bet we look good now, no? And now that you have your rights you can sit back and enjoy the privileged life. Tell us what to do so we can be just like you. Hmph. You don't even know how privileged you are. Well, we are not so fortunate."

"Uh, yes you are," Charlene said incredulous. "Look around you. You go to one of the most prestigious schools in the state. You have access to food, clean water, the Internet. You are surrounded by open-minded people who generally want to help you succeed. You're making it seem like you're living in Afghanistan or a ravaged war zone in Syria."

An African-American girl wearing a headband sat up in her chair and started to freak out.

"I'm black and I'm trans. Everywhere I go I might as well be walking through a village in Yemen. You don't get it, do you? They want to kill us!"

"Who wants to kill you?" Charlene asked.

"Them," G said. "If we don't weed out those who want to see us silenced, then **we** are most certainly good as dead,"

The African-American trans girl smiled in satisfaction upon hearing G's words. She felt validated. She would now follow G to whatever end awaited.

"You do realize you're leaving out quite a few groups from your name?" G said while pointing at the Pride Flag hanging from the table.

"We try to be as inclusive as possible."

"Sure, with the 'L' coming first."

"What do you suggest, then? The letter 'G' instead?"

"A new acronym. It will take some time to memorize it and take it to heart: LGGBDTTTIQQAAPP+"

"I don't even know what all of those letters represent," Charlene said exasperated.

"You will. And you will come to understand this: We did not choose these circumstances, but we will certainly make history from it, and create something new that has never existed before."

Charlene nodded. Realizing that the Alliance was now being co-opted by the Collective, she backed off her attack. She knew this was a fight she could no longer win. Anything she'd say would be shot down by radical forces who had become adept at blocking every single argument by using postmodernist doublespeak.

She would instead retreat and seek the counsel of Karen Francis.

Chapter 10

Mondel lingered at the student government meeting for another half hour. Chance demanded to know what he, Mondel, was going to do if G was going to ignore him. It honestly never crossed anyone's mind. If G forced the college's hand, they could conceivably expel her.

Returning to his office, he poured himself a stiff shot of Jameson from the bottle in his desk. He needed to think. The Professor would not be happy. He'd demand to know what had happened and how he could've screwed up such an impossibly simple task. Mondel desperately searched his mind for a solution, but the options were limited.

"Dr. Mondel, Professor Papadopoulos on line one," called Dana from the other room.

Mondel looked at the flashing light on the phone.

"Thanks Dana," he said exhaling and picking up.

"What the fuck happened?" demanded P.

"She won't accept the punishment," explained Mondel. "She said she doesn't recognize the authority of the student government."

"Is she crazy? She'll force the school to expel her! Did you tell her that?!"

"We never got that far in the conversation. They just protested, chanted a bunch of nonsense, called us all fascists and marched out," explained Mondel.

As Mondel talked, Wes walked into the room. He waved, then immediately sat down in front of his computer and started typing. Mondel acknowledged him but held a finger aloft to indicate he needed a second.

"Well fuck that little cunt!" growled the professor. "That shit stain thinks she can push back on us? Okay. Fuck. I'm going to have to take this to Albert. You just sit tight and for God's sake, don't say anything to anyone. The last thing we need is this exploding on the Internet."

As Mondel listened, Wes summoned Twitter on the laptop screen and logged into his account. He found a short video that was being shared. It featured Mondel in a clip saying, "That's Fascism!" But it was presented out of context, not like he was knocking it, but like he was explaining some wacky sitcom premise. He looked at the stats below. The meeting had ended less than an hour ago and it had already been shared 40,000 times.

"I have to go," said Mondel, hanging up while staring at the screen.

The video was already being altered and shared. Someone had created a deep fake, plastering Hitler's face over his. In another version, someone had put a Nazi uniform over his body and altered his hand movement so it looked like he was doing the Hitler salute. In addition, GIFs and memes were being made including ones of G looking triumphant and being hailed as "Milkshake Girl". They photoshopped her into Daenerys Targaryen from Game of Thrones and called her "Breaker of Chains, Thrower of Milkshakes!"

"I'm sorry, buddy," said Wes, grimly. "I thought you should see it as soon as possible."

"I'm so unbelievably fucked," muttered Mondel.

"Not necessarily," Wes said, trying to give him hope. "You're Jewish, so this could technically be a hate crime."

"They're going to fire me," Mondel said, rubbing his eyes. "I'm going to be fired."

"You've got tenure, they can't fire you," Wes concluded. "Although I guess they could buy you out or let you go and make you sue for your money."

"How does this happen?" asked Mondel aghast. "The speaker was a Centrist."

"But he supported Trump, right?"

"No!"

"Hey, I'm on your side, take it easy," Wes concluded. "You got any vacation time coming your way?"

"I burned it all during the divorce and then some," Mondel admitted. "I promised P I wouldn't take a day for at least the next two years."

"Look, maybe you get out ahead of this," suggested Wes. "Present it in your class as one big joke and laugh it off."

"When's the last time you felt comfortable telling a joke in class?"

"Mmm, 2015," admitted Wes, after thinking about it.

"I can't avoid this, Wes," Mondel thought aloud. "I mean, shit, this is what I **teach**."

Wes helped himself to the bottle and poured them both a shot.

"Wait a minute, that kid, the cartoonist--- What's his name? I think we have him both in a class," Wes said trying to remember.

"Tyler Brown?" Mondel recalled. "What about him?"

"He's a cartoonist. Get him to do a cartoon or a meme or something," explained Wes. "Kids are always creating memes. They love them."

"What do you call that?" Mondel said, gesturing to the screen and his repeating image.

"Yeah, but that was made by one of those Antifa assholes. Get one of the conservative kids to do it. They're great at memes!" concluded Wes.

"Conservative kids? Who?" griped Mondel. "I'm in the Political Science department and I don't even know any."

"There must be some," Wes insisted. "On a campus this size, how could there not be?"

"I don't think countering the narrative is going to help," Mondel dismissed.

In the next room, Mondel could hear Dana scolding someone.

"I'm sorry, you can't just go in there. Dr. Mondel!" Dana said.

A student was headed for the doorway. Mondel and Wes hid their drinks.

"Dr. Mondel, Upstate Tribune, we'd like to get a statement," said the pushy student.

"And you are?"

"Carl Gravas, I'm doing a feature on the incident," he explained, taking out his phone and starting the app.

"I have nothing to say on camera or on the record," said Mondel. "No comment right now."

Dana got to the doorway.

"I'm sorry, Dr. Mondel, he just barged in."

"It's fine, Dana," Mondel assured. "But seriously, you'll have to go."

Carl turned off his phone and pocketed it.

"Okay, I get it. You have a job and a family," he said, taking a different tact. "But if you don't give a statement, this will just keep getting worse. I'm not asking you to make an **official** statement from yourself or the college. I just have a few qualifying questions to ask you. They're just about facts and I promise you no one will know that I talked to you. I protect my sources."

"He's good," insisted Wes, trying to brush him off. "You can leave."

"What's your question?" asked Mondel out of curiosity.

"Are you now or have you ever been a member of the Nazi Party, Dr. Mondel?"

Chapter 11

"I'm Jewish!" Mondel said, incredulous.

"So you claim to be Jewish," Carl noted.

"No! That's not a claim! I'm a Jew! That's an objective fact!"

"Well, reality is to a large extent, subjective. If you read Foucault---"

"Get out! And I know who Foucault is!" insisted Mondel. "I have no comment!"

"Can I get your name?" Carl asked Wes.

"I'm just the IT guy here to fix the computer," lied Wes. "You're all set, doc. If you have any other problems, let me know."

Wes made a hasty retreat. Carl lingered, looking around the offices.

"Go," Mondel insisted.

"Hey, my parents paid for this," pointed out Carl. "Technically, **you** work for **me**."

"Go!" yelled Mondel, losing his cool.

As Carl left, Tyler Brown walked in. He noted the student reporter as he exited.

"Tyler," Mondel said in relief. "What can I do for you?"

"Everything okay?" asked Tyler.

"Campus reporter," dismissed the doctor.

"Yeah, Carl's a douche," Tyler recalled. "I actually wanted to show you some political cartoons I've been working on. Get your opinion."

The doctor's heart leapt. This was exactly what he needed! Wes called it! If another student defended him, perhaps he could fight the narrative.

"There's this cartoon called the Bechdel Test about movies," explained Tyler. "Well I did one called the Mondel Test, after you."

"Wow, that's great!" Mondel said excitedly. "I'm flattered!"

Tyler handed him the piece of paper with the cartoon. It was a parody of the Bechdel Test in that instead of two women walking out of a movie theater and talking about the films they would watch, it was two college age guys. The conversation mostly mirrored the one Tyler had had in dorm lounge about going to see movies with more titties and bush. Mondel forced a smile. Well, at least he was the only one to see the cartoon. Right?

"Things are a little interesting for me at the college right now," Mondel tried to explain. "Wait, you didn't post this, did you?"

"Oh, yeah," Tyler said cheerfully. "Almost ten thousand upvotes on Reddit. They love it!"

The doctor sighed. Oh, well. At least at this point, it couldn't get much worse. Mondel did his best to plant the meme seed in Tyler's head, but he was careful not to give him direct orders to do it. The last thing he needed was one of his good students getting pilloried for defending him and then blaming him for the backlash.

The whole day was just a little too much to take.

Mondel had to get away from campus and the students. He walked to K lot where he parked his car. Along the way, he remembered meeting Brianna on the stretch of sidewalk while walking to class...

He was trying to figure out his schedule while looking at the carbon copied list when he bumped into her. It was meet cute.

"Oh, I'm sorry," Mondel had said to her.

"My mistake," she said. "I should've been looking."

"I'm Lawrence," he introduced.

"Brianna," she replied.

And that was it. They dated, fell in love, got married, had a kid--- Shared a life for a while. That was the magic of being on campus.

He was reminded of all of this when he spotted two students on roughly the same trajectory. The girl was looking at her phone and the guy had looked away. They bumped into each other.

"Oh, I'm sorry," he said to her in the exact same way.

"Did you just try to feel me up?!" the woman snapped, accusing him.

"What? No!" he replied. "You were the one looking at your phone. You ran into me."

"Stop victim shaming! What you just did was practically **rape**!" she threatened.

"You're crazy," he said walking away.

"Don't disparage the mentally disabled!" she shouted at him.

56

The girl looked his way. Mondel avoided her gaze and got into his car.

Driving back to his apartment, he entered as his phone rang. It was Brianna.

"Hey, it's funny you called," he said. "I was just passing by K Lot thinking---"

"Lawrence, have you seen the Internet? What is happening on campus?" she demanded. "What did you do?"

"I didn't do anything," he explained. "It's a long story. Do you really want to hear it?"

"If it impacts Zoe? Yes!" she insisted.

"I don't think it would, but fine," Mondel relented. "We had a freshman throw a milkshake at a speaker. The student government was supposed to discipline her and in the meeting, she kept correcting everyone's language. I said that that was fascism because they were calling everyone a fascist."

"What?" she said not understanding. "That doesn't make any sense."

"I know," Mondel agreed, completely frustrated.

"Well, they shouldn't be allowed to use your image like that!" Brianna insisted. "You have to stand up to them, Lawrence!"

"Stand up to who?" he asked. "Have you **been** on the Internet? Plus these are college students we're talking about."

"Zoe is in high school, Lawrence," Brianna whined. "She's a very sensitive girl."

"You can't keep helicoptering her, Bri!" snapped Mondel. "The world can be a dark place! She needs to know that!"

"Don't start this argument again!" Brianna yelled, the old wounds tearing open. "She was nearly **kidnapped** by that child predator!"

"The cops were talking about a sex offender that moved into the neighborhood! They have to do that by law! I told you!" Mondel insisted.

"He prowled the streets! They said!"

"The cops were on top of it! That was the whole point of the visit! Why do you keep rewriting history?"

"You didn't want to move!" she accused, starting to cry.

"To where? There are sex offenders in every town, every neighborhood, everywhere! I showed you the fucking map online! If we just teach our kid to be smart, alert and tough---"

"I can't handle this conversation anymore! I'm taking a Valium and going to bed!" she cried. "I hope you're happy!"

Brianna hung up and Mondel was alone again. Their divorce was for the best. After Zoe was born, Brianna would spiral into drama scenarios. She was afraid of going to cities, afraid of meeting new people, afraid for Zoe, afraid for him--- The dozens of worried phone calls, the redundant security plans, constant checking in--- The cops talking about the sex offender had set her on tilt. Mondel spent thousands on a home security system that Brianna was constantly setting off. It was motion sensitive, but she'd turn it on and sit still in the house "just to be safe".

No amount of convincing could get her to a therapist. At his whit's end, he eventually asked for a divorce if she wouldn't go. She took it as a sign that she could move to a "safe" area. Now she lived in a house in the middle of the woods, driving Zoe thirty minutes one way to school. She was probably terribly lonely, but Mondel guessed she was secure in her mind at least. The house was going to feel very empty when Zoe moved on, but at least that wouldn't be his problem anymore.

Getting on his laptop at home, Mondel logged into his Twitter account. He was flooded with notifications. The first four were from friends and family from two years ago, the last time he really used it. The rest were angry insults and forwards of the video.

He tried his best to figure out who had originally posted it, but it was impossible. He wasn't a computer guy and he definitely wasn't a social media guy. The comments were a nightmare of insults that ran the gamut from Anti-Semitic to clever puns based on his name. Mondel wondered who these people were that had so much free time to yell at a stranger. Were their own lives that empty?

After a lonely dinner and way too much time on the Internet, his phone buzzed. It was a text from the professor: "The bar. Now."

Mondel replied "K", hopped in his car and headed into town. The sun had set and it was after hours in the middle of the week. The garage was free and he could park on the first floor. He passed Homeless Vic, who was heading home for the night.

"Hey Vic," he greeted. "All I have is a dollar. Sorry."

"Oh, hey, don't beat yourself up, doc," he dismissed. "You're my dawg! You're my niggah! You've always been! What's wrong?"

"Craziness on campus," said Mondel. "Plus there's a picture of me going around the Internet."

"A naked one?" asked Vic, trying to understand.

"No-no. Something I said taken out of context. It's all over Twitter."

"Twitter?" laughed Vic. "Those college kids live on that. That ain't the real world! **This** is the real world!"

Vic pointed to his bundle which was a trash bag full of clothes jammed inside a metal cart.

"Send some of them students my way," he offered. "I'll show them what really goes down on the streets. This town is crazy sometimes! You don't even know!"

Mondel laughed at the thought, although it was probably the wake up call most of them needed.

Walking into the tavern, he found the professor in a booth far to the right, away from the other patrons. They were watching a football game, but Papadopoulos was in a more quiet space.

"You saw the Internet?" Mondel greeted.

"Everyone sees the Internet, so yeah," he acknowledged.

"I'm so sorry, Professor," he apologized.

"Fuck that. You think I give a shit about that?" he dismissed, nodding to the bartender for another round. "If I gave a flying fuck what those pissants on Twitter thought, I would've blown out my brains a long time ago. Jack Dorsey should be hung up by his balls."

The bartender came by with P's drink. Mondel ordered a soda.

"What is happening?" Mondel said, a bit lost. "Is society unraveling?"

"Hmm, maybe," acknowledged the prof. "Maybe we just live in a dying Empire and are unfortunate enough to live long enough to die with it."

"I have a daughter," Mondel said. "What kind of world is this? Where's the normal now?"

"It is what it is, Lawrence," P said somberly. "But I do have some good news, as well as bad news."

"What's the good news?" Mondel said hopefully.

"I explained to Albert what happened as best I could, but he is a clueless fuck that thinks it's no big deal," said the professor, turning his glass. "That keeps us out of the line of fire for now, but he wants to have a **meeting** about it at some point."

"At some point?" repeated Mondel. "She's completely ignoring the student government. They look like laughing stocks, we look ineffectual."

"I agree, but he does not care how we look, so long as the school keeps churning out degrees," explained P. "He's also frozen the student government's money until G either capitulates or until things calm down."

"Well, I guess that's something, although that's sure not going to make the other students happy," Mondel figured. "Wait, what's the bad news?"

"He wants to plan an event for next year."

Mondel couldn't believe it. The tone deaf dean must've been too isolated in his house to understand what was going on. What could possibly be more important than disciplining his own unruly students?

"What event?"

Professor P looked at him somberly. In that moment, they both knew just how oblivious the Dean really was to the sensibilities of the modern college student.

"Columbus Day."

Chapter 12

The next morning, Mondel had his Legislative Process and Public Policy class along with another Poly-Sci 101 class. This time, three students had dropped out of the 101 class and one of the upper classman hadn't showed up.

On the way to his office Mondel crossed paths with the reason why. G and her minions had organized a protest in front of the Student Union. About two dozen college kids, supported by black clad Antifa members, were carrying signs and chanting. Mondel recognized some of the trans women athletes as well as members of the LGBTQ community. They had a huge flag with the letters "PBC" and some of the students were showing off new tattoos with the acronym in a logo. It was a red background with bright yellow letters. They had signs that said #FreeG and #HelpMilkshakeGirl. One of the students had a sign with a printed image from the video clip of Mondel with the caption, "That's Fascism!"

Mondel decided to ignore the protest and walk past, until he spotted a familiar face amongst the students. Fawkes was talking to the group and encouraging them. For Mondel, this was a bridge too far. It was one thing to support students in their activities, but it was another to support activities that would actively tear down a colleague's career. He approached Fawkes, hoping the students wouldn't notice him.

"Can I talk to you for a moment, **professor**?" Mondel asked in a measured tone.

"Dr. Mondel!" Fawkes said in a normal voice, not modulating at all. "Isn't this great?!"

"No, it's not great!" Mondel muttered. "Do you see the sign they have?"

The girl holding the sign looked up at the picture and then Mondel. She finally realized who was standing there.

"Hey! It's Fascism Guy!" she said pointing. "Boo! Boo! Fascism!"

The other protesters began realizing who he was and started to surround him.

"Fascist!" screamed another student.

"I'm not a fascist!" Mondel insisted. "I've been a Liberal my whole life!"

"Boo! Liberal! Boo!" booed a student in the back of the mob.

"Liberals get the bullet too!" added one of the Antifa kids, who then laughed with the rest.

"That is completely uncalled for, young man!" chastised Mondel.

"You don't know what gender I identify!" snapped back the Antifa kid.

"Political violence is completely wrong!" Mondel assured the crowd. "History proves that it just leads to more violence."

"Tell that to the girl in Charlottesville!" countered the Antifa member.

"What? That doesn't address the point at all!" Mondel said.

Chloe, a trans woman athlete with enormously broad shoulders, stepped forward. She had recently shattered the campus record for shot putting. Getting right into his face, she shouted at him in a very baritone voice.

"Your fascism and transphobia aren't welcomed on this campus! Ever!"

The protesters cheered and Mondel froze. He felt like the crowd was going to lynch him at any minute and that the shot putter might actually punch his face in. She shook with rage when she said the word "Ever!"

"Fawkes, will you please tell these students that I am not a fascist?!" he gritted through his teeth as calmly as he could.

"Guys, he's not a fascist," assured Fawkes.

Chloe and the rest of the mob started to relax a little. Mondel felt his pulse finally start to slow to normal levels.

"But he is a tool of the Patriarchy," continued Fawkes. "I mean, he is a white cis male, like me so duh! We obviously can't trust him, but he just a cog in the Capitalistic system that continues to oppress us all."

"Patriarchal tool!" raged Chloe before walking away.

"We have a meeting," Mondel reminded Fawkes. "In about ten minutes."

"Oh, yeah," Fawkes suddenly remembered. "Keep the fires burning everyone! You're doing great!"

Fawkes made the black power salute and then started walking toward the offices with Mondel.

"Have you lost your mind?" Mondel asked him as they headed for the faculty building.

"What?" said Fawkes.

"We're trying to calm this situation and you're encouraging the students to protest!" said Mondel.

"It's their right to protest. It's about Freedom of Speech," pointed out Fawkes.

Mondel looked back. One of the students held a sign that said, "No Free Speech for Nazis!" and another had one that said "Deplatform Fascists!"

"What do you call that?!" demanded Mondel, pointing at the signs.

"You said you didn't want violence. Speech **is** violence sometimes," said Fawkes knowingly.

"When? When was that ever the case, Fawkes? Do you even hear yourself?!" Mondel ranted. "Look at what's happening!"

"All I see is the exercise of Freedom of Speech," he said proudly.

One of the students was burning a sign that said, "Free Speech". An Antifa member knocked it to the ground and everyone started stomping on it.

"Look at what they're doing! They don't care about Freedom of Speech!" insisted Mondel. "You can't keep encouraging this!"

"Hey, those students are from some pretty marginalized groups," countered Fawkes. "And there are white supremacists, white nationalists, Nazis, fascists, Trump Supporters, Republicans, the Christian Right, far right, alt-right--- They're all against them."

Mondel stopped him and looked him in the eye. He wanted to see if Fawkes was just as crazy as the students.

"Almost **none** of the people you just mentioned have ever set foot on this campus!" Mondel said to him seriously. "And as for Republicans and Trump Supporters, you could probably count both on the fingers of **one** hand!"

"They're still **here**," pointed out Fawkes weakly.

"How does that make the protesters marginalized, Fawkes?!" snapped Mondel. "They've got me on a sign! They're calling me the Fascism Guy!"

"**You** brought the fascist to campus," Fawkes reminded him.

"**Centrist**! He was a centrist!" yelled Mondel.

"Ladies, if you don't mind," Professor P said, poking his head out of the office door. "We have to get this started."

Most of the faculty had gathered in a lecture hall in the faculty building. The Dean was calling in on video conference. His giant face was projected on the front wall. He was sitting in his comfortable and finely appointed living room with his Shih Tzu on his lap.

"Hello everyone!" he greeted cheerfully. "Thank you all for coming and let me say a special thanks to Dr. Mondel for handling our recent speaker."

The Dean applauded him and the rest of the faculty applauded in agreement weakly. Mondel was unsure whether or not he should take the praise. Professor P gestured with his hand for him to let it go.

"Now first, I wanted to address the thing in the bookstore," the Dean began. "Gwendolyn?"

Gwen from Carving and Fiber Art Studies, stood up to address the Dean.

"The students are not buying enough of our books," she complained. "We spent three years writing that and they're just selling it back to each other or copying it online! We need a new edition!"

"Well, Gwen, how much has changed in Carving and Fiber Arts?" asked the Dean. "I mean, really?"

At this point, Franklin came in late. The Professor and Mondel talked him in whispers while the meeting continued.

"Where were you?" asked Professor P.

"I was on the phone with New Teen Trend," smiled Franklin excitedly. "They're doing an article about Karl Marx and wanted my input."

"New Teen Trend?" asked Mondel. "My daughter reads New Teen Trend. It's a makeup magazine."

"They're doing some very forward work there," said Franklin cheerfully. "They're showing young people just how relevant Marx can be today!"

"He's been dead for over a century," Mondel said, aghast.

"Mondel, ideas never die," chuckled Franklin. "You should know that."

For the next twenty minutes, the Dean took in the petty complaints of the faculty. Most of them were about books or other accessories and how to get the students to buy more of them. If you had asked one of the professors if they cared about the money, they would've considered the question in the poorest of taste. But when it came to complaining about it to the Dean, nothing was too shameless. After all, reprinting a book or new edition came out of the college's pocket, not theirs. They just got the royalty. The Dean had, of course, co-authored or edited several of the books himself.

"I would also like to congratulate Professor Fawkes," said the Dean. "He just got published in the academic journal, Political Perspectives. The article was called Applications of Marxism on Tinder."

Mondel and Diana looked at Professor P. He just shook his head sadly. Franklin started the applause and the rest of the room followed.

"How did you have time to write an academic paper this semester?" whispered Mondel.

"It's easy," dismissed Fawkes. "Banged it out in a weekend while I was binging Better Call Saul."

The paper, of course, didn't really matter. Almost no one read these academic journals. They piled up in the library collecting dust. The only person who'd assign reading the article would be Fawkes and he wrote so many, he'd be onto the next one in a few weeks. Just another pay day and the college loved the perceived prestige of more published work, even though they paid for it all. Mondel wondered what the regents would say if they new the true costs of the money they were pouring into books and articles no one ever was meant to read.

"Some more great news I know you'll be excited about," said the Dean, anticipating. "My good friend, General Kensington, helped me push through a whopping federal grant to build a new, state-of-the-art computer lab for the college! This will expand the Computer Science Department! Our students will be developing the AI that will be inside drones!"

Mondel looked at Wes, who shifted uncomfortably in his seat. He raised his hand.

"Yes, Wesley?" recognized the Dean.

"Sir, I'm a little wary of the application of developing artificial intelligence for weapons," he said gingerly.

"It's an emerging field with massive job potential, I'm told," the Dean explained. "Plus the entire Science Department would be expanded, including some raises, of course."

"Oh," said Wes, backing off.

Wes suddenly started doing the math in his head on how fast he might finally be able to afford that jetski. It was not like he was going to be teaching it, so morally, he felt fine with it.

"M-m-maybe the students might have some moral objection to the program, sir," said Mondel, trying to insert himself into the discussion. "Because it sounds like work for the Pentagon."

"Department of Defense," corrected the Dean as if that were way different. "I'm told the human pilots make so many mistakes with drones, this could really solve that."

"But---"

The Dean moved on. Whether he was oblivious to the impact of the research or the students' reaction, Mondel couldn't tell. Ultimately, he was just a money vacuum for the college. By hook or by crook, he'd expand it, add more students and make the college bigger and better. Isn't that what deans were supposed to do?

"So next year, we're going to institute the Quad Learning program," explained the Dean. "Four classes, four instructors, combined into one class."

Mondel made eye contact with Wes. He rolled his eyes at the Quad Learning idea.

"Now I have a few pitches for next year," said the Dean, checking his phone. "Political Theater With Sports Related Injuries. This course studies the political science of theater and how it impacts themes related to sports and biology."

Rubbing his temple, Mondel prayed he wouldn't be picked to be a part of that word salad. He spotted Celia across the way and she made a joking gesture that he and she would be teaching the course. Mondel smiled despite himself.

"See it combines our Political Science, Theater, Sports Medicine and Biology classes all in one," the Dean said excitedly. "We just have to find some political plays with sports injuries in them or write them. Maybe plant a seed in the heads of your writing students, professors."

Leaning over to Professor P, Mondel whispered, "He's serious about this?"

"Oh, fuck yes," replied P. "Fortunately, just because we offer the class doesn't mean anyone will sign up for it. Even our students aren't that stupid."

"Okay, before I wrap this up, I just wanted to talk about our event for next year," the Dean said proudly. "Columbus Day on Campus! It has it all! History, Science, Diversity!"

"Sir, if I may," offered up the chair from the History Department. "The holiday itself is considered insensitive to indigenous peoples. Perhaps an Indigenous Peoples Day?"

"What? No," said the Dean confused. "You have it all wrong. Columbus Day itself was a celebration of Italian-American heritage. It was founded by an Italian immigrant in 1909 and pushed through legislation by a Hispanic State Senator in the same year! You can't get more diverse than that."

Mondel looked at P again. He just shook his head, exhausted at the thought of retelling how he tried to convince the Dean not to pursue the event.

"Trust me, once the students see things--- Well, you'll explain the history to them--- They'll get on board," assured the Dean. "Now I hate to cut this short, but I have a meeting with the regents. Keep up the good work everyone!"

Chapter 13

A week had passed since the protest in front of the Student Union. The general feeling on the campus of Upstate College was of total ill ease. Classes were still taking place, but many departments were facing multiple issues.

A professor teaching biology had several students refuse to accept his lecture on human anatomy. He had expected some pushback, particularly by those who purported that humans are not actually born male or female, but are rather "blank slates" and they can become any gender they so choose as they develop, or morph laterally or cross-laterally whenever need be. But that wasn't the problem in their minds. The real issue the students had was with the notion that science, to them at least, was a modern Western construct, based on imperialistic European style ideas. It didn't account for other thought processes from different parts of the world, such as Africa and Asia, and thus was racist.

"We need to shelve all science as it stands and start over," one student demanded. "If we begin again with a level playing field, taking into account voices from every continent, every race, creed, and gender, we can implement decolonization and form a basis for a properly calibrated research system. We can actually do it right this time."

The professor, backed into a corner, with the eyes of his students fully fixed on him for an answer, let go of all reason. Years of hard work, study and diligent preparation were tossed aside to placate a growing outrage.

"You might be onto something…"

In a Sociology class four students claimed that the pop quiz they were given was problematic.

"We can't take this test," said the student. "We had no idea you were going to give it!"

"Yes!" agreed the second. "Surprises are a total trigger!"

Several other members of the class, agreed. No one had studied for the test, which was sort of the point.

"You don't get to decide when I give tests," said the professor, carefully. "I'm sorry you're unprepared."

"Now, you're triggering me!" added a student. "What is this? Nazi Germany?!"

At the same time, Plato's Allegory of the Cave was deconstructed in a philosophy class by a rather precarious student.

"How can I take the struggle of the prisoners seriously if they're all white?"

"Well, the Greeks really didn't have a term for 'white' back then," said the female professor. "In fact, they didn't see race at all like we do. They actually portrayed white skin as being attuned to someone's gender. Women were supposed to stay inside and out of the sun, so they were depicted as being paler. Men worked outside and tanned, so in their imagery the men appear black."

"So the Greeks were patriarchal scum and misogynists!" the student cried out. "That's even worse, don't you see, professor? The Allegory of the Cave is even more problematic than we had once thought."

"I'm not sure who this 'we' is you are referencing. And besides, Plato's work has been studied for thousands of years and it's the basis for---"

"For capitalism, right? Oh please, professor! If you're not a part of the solution you're colluding with the problem!"

"There's no collusion!" the professor shouted.

Meanwhile, in a building in an area of the campus peppered by old oak trees, with a small park nearby, one complete with a statue garden, the Theater Department faced its own crisis...

Celia was in rehearsal with her drama students for the spring play, M. Butterfly. Dylan Walsh, a senior who had the lead in many past productions, was cast as René Gallimard.

In the play Gallimard is a member of the French Embassy in China and becomes infatuated with an opera singer, Song Liling. He views her as an example of the perfect woman only to find out much later on she is actually a man. The role of Song Liling was to be played by a female student, an Asian-American named Shino Yawen.

Preparations had been going well up until after the protest. Since then, quiet rumblings amongst the cast and crew members could be heard. On this day, however, those voices had become even louder. So much so Celia had to address them. She gathered everyone up in the seats nearest to the stage but decided to speak with them from the walkway in front of it, rather than from the stage itself. To be on the same page, as equals, or so she thought.

"I understand there are some concerns about the production," Celia said to the group. "I know there's a lot going on right now, but I want to give you a platform to speak your mind so we can sort through whatever issues you might have and move on with the show."

Autumn, a sophomore with dyed black hair and a red streak, raised her hand.

"You are welcome to tell us your thoughts, Autumn," Celia said with an understanding smile.

"Professor Lilywater, I think I can speak for everyone and say we'd like to fix the play," Autumn said.

Celia was immediately taken aback by this. She expected some criticisms of the performances and perhaps some suggestions for scheduling adjustments, but this was entirely something else. She knew she would have to tread carefully with her response.

"Ok. Can you explain your concerns further?"

"Oh, we plan to," Autumn said with a defiant flair. "First, Dylan is a sexual abuser and needs to be removed from the play."

Dylan, who was sitting to the side texting on his phone, looked up upon hearing his name. When he realized what was said he shifted to a defensive position.

"Now Autumn, that sort of accusation---" began Celia.

"I am not a fucking sexual abuser!" Dylan proclaimed.

"You violate Shino's space," Autumn said.

"What? How?"

Now Shino was drawn into the conversation. She shifted uneasily in her white ruffled blouse and black pencil skirt. She clearly didn't want to be involved.

"Did you ask her permission to kiss her?"

"It's part of the role," Dylan said exasperated.

"So you just assumed you could violate her space?"

"It's called acting!"

Autumn turned to Shino.

"Did Dylan ask you if it was permissible to touch you?"

"I don't understand---" Shino said with a confused look on her face.

"Yeah, did he?" asked the costume designer for the play.

"Well, no, but---"

"So he didn't," Autumn said confirming it in her mind while also solidifying the accusation amongst many in the group.

"This is a slippery slope," Celia said. "It is important for us to listen to accusers, but Shino isn't---"

"Well, wait-a-second," Shino said.

Dylan couldn't believe what was happening. He started to break out in a cold sweat and stood up to try and regain control of the narrative.

"Shino, you don't honestly believe this, do you?"

"Well, why didn't you ask me, first? Did you just think you automatically could because…"

"Yeah, why did you attack her agency?" Autumn asked with a growing feverous furor. "Do you think that just because you're a cis man you can make those choices for her?"

Shino was starting to believe this train of thought and began to get emotional. Celia noticed this and decided to make a desperate play to rein the group in.

"We'll look into these accusations," she said.

Autumn dialed it back and crossed her arms.

"Good. We have some other thoughts as well."

Dylan was pacing back and forth now.

"Are you serious? You're going to listen to them? What am I, a suspect or something now?"

"Just give me a moment," Celia said trying to keep a lid on the situation. She closed her eyes and took a deep breath.

"I didn't do anything. I'm an actor--- it was acting!" Dylan exclaimed.

Autumn was standing up with a legal pad in hand. She had other notes prepared.

"We have other demands, Professor," she said.

She then heard the door to the auditorium slam. Dylan had stormed out.

"Well, that solves one of them: Remove Dylan Walsh from the lead role," Autumn said using her pen to cross out the line on the legal pad. "Secondly, we'd like to recast Song Liling's part with a genderqueer actor."

Shino looked horrified, but what could she do?

"I'm fine with that," Shino said through tears.

"Are you sure, Shino?" Celia asked.

"Yes, Professor Lilywater. I don't want to cause any issues. A genderqueer person should play the part," Shino said while wiping her eyes. "Maybe I could…paint the set."

"Thirdly," Autumn said before a pause. "Thirdly we'd like to make some alterations to the script."

"Wait, what?" Celia was accepting of the casting changes but this was crossing a moral, ethical and artistic line for her.

"Much of what is written is very problematic," Autumn insisted.

"M. Butterfly was nominated for a Pulitzer Prize! It's a Tony Award Winning play!"

70

"But is it really? Who decided that? Privileged cisgender white people, right?"

"It's a modern classic!" Celia cried out to seemingly deaf ears.

Autumn crossed her arms. The cast and crew were unified behind her. If there was a voice of dissent they didn't dare speak out now.

"Well, I can't allow you to change it," Celia said firmly.

"You don't get to tell us anything," Autumn said. "Besides, we already rewrote it."

She produced a binder with loose leaf pages inside. The cover had the title Mx Butterfly in big black hand-drawn letters.

"In the new version Song is never submissive and exercises their agency at all times. They're able to get the information they need from Gallimard to help further the cause of Communism in France. In the end they become a leader in the movement to make Europe a better place for all people. A truly Socialistic unified state."

Celia felt a cold chill. She knew she had lost her own power. If she wanted to remain involved at all she'd had to take a backseat. Autumn was running the show now.

"Ok, I understand," Celia said and nodded. "I need a moment."

"Very well," Autumn said. "We're going to choose someone to play Song right now. There are three genderqueer actors in the group. Did you know that?"

"Thank you for informing me," Celia replied. She knew better than to answer any questions directly right now, whether she knew the answer or not.

She walked up to the doors and pulled them open. They seemed heavier than before. In the hallway outside the theater Mondel was pacing about.

"Celia!" he called out to her.

She barely registered he was there.

"I need to talk with you in person," he said smiling. "I was thinking of taking you to dinner at the Concord on Friday. It's a bit of a drive, but they have a jazz quartet and an amazing wine bar that---"

"Now is not a good time," she said.

"Oh, what's wrong?" he asked concerned that he had misread her in the moment. "You worried you're going to have to teach a class with me?"

"The students--- They're changing the play and--- Well, it's something I'm just going to have to accept. I think it's going to require more of my time, however, so…"

"Oh. Okay, sure. I can understand that."

71

He didn't, really. So much about the behavior of women had always puzzled him. He often wondered if anyone had the answers. If they did, perhaps they weren't sharing.

"So are we putting a pause on…everything?" he asked, trying to decipher the tea leaves.

She looked up him hopefully and bit her thumb in anticipation of his response.

"Yes, of course," he said calmly. "Take all the time that you need."

She let out a sigh and then took a deep breath.

"Thank you, Lawrence. I'll explain more when I can. I have to get back to my students."

Celia turned and walked towards the auditorium. Mondel almost forgot his manners and then raced to open the door for her. As he stood there holding it she walked under his arm and into the theater without so much as thanking him. He thought it was strange, but everything about this encounter had baffled him.

Chapter 14

Daily protests were becoming a thing on campus at this point. Whenever anyone walked on the quad now, they expected to see students carrying placards, marching and chanting. It was like the college had become a testing ground for political radicals.

Today's protest was against the Thanksgiving Day mural in Jefferson Hall. The piece of art, painted in the late 30's, depicted the Pilgrims sharing a Thanksgiving dinner with the local natives. The mural was the only piece of historically relevant artwork on the campus. Despite the fact it was called "Sharing the Meal" and was meant to depict togetherness with the new and old world, the students insisted it was a hateful reminder of bigotry, colonialism and, since one of the Native Americans in the mural was heavyset, fat-shaming. The protesters had duct taped sheets over the mural, which confused passerbys, as it covered the very thing they were protesting.

Mondel hated going to campus now. What he had loved as a student and as a new professor, the constant protesting had made him sour on. He was tired of checking his language and his privilege during his interactions with the students. It was like being in a mental prison that made him walk on eggshells.

Daniel Voss, a History grad student he had taught, called him with an urgent plea. Normally, Mondel would've been happy to meet him and counsel him, but the T.A. needed to convene in the library on campus for some reason. Even though Mondel wanted to hide in his apartment and forget about work, he made the trek back to the library to greet him in person. He found him on the third floor in the science fiction section.

"Thanks for meeting me," Daniel said.

"Why couldn't we meet downtown or something?" asked Mondel.

"I can't risk this getting out and no one comes up here anymore," he said, keeping his voice low. "I think I'm being MeToo'd and I don't know what to do!"

"What? Who?" asked Mondel.

"My girlfriend, Alyssa," he whispered.

"Alyssa? You've been dating her awhile, haven't you?"

"More than two years," he explained. "She's graduating this year."

"I don't understand, what is she saying you did?"

"She says that I took advantage of my position as a teaching assistant to make her have a relationship with me!" hissed Daniel. "But we were dating before I even got the job and moved on to grad school!"

"I think you're okay, Daniel," Mondel guessed. "I mean, you were students together. Why did she bring this up now?"

"It's Milkshake Girl!" he insisted, the stress showing on his face. "She's got her convinced that everything I do is oppressing her! I love her doc, but Alyssa's changed!"

"Look, people change," suggested Mondel. "Maybe it's time you break it off for a while. Give yourselves both time to think."

"I don't know," he said, a bit despondent. "She says if I confess what I did, then all would be forgiven."

"Confess? It sounds like a religion," said Mondel. "Listen to me, whatever you do--- Don't confess anything. Do you hear me?"

"But she said---"

"Daniel, if you didn't do anything, you have nothing to be sorry for," insisted Mondel. "You shouldn't confess to things you didn't do just to appease someone."

"Okay," he said, still a little shaky. "Thanks doc. I appreciate it."

Mondel moved to walk out of the book section with him, but Daniel put up his hand.

"Doc, would you mind waiting so people don't see us leave together," he requested. "I hate to ask, but there are a lot of protesters outside."

Mondel nodded sadly and let Daniel go. He looked at the shelves and picked up a copy of Fahrenheit 451.

"A classic," he muttered.

As he flipped through the pages, he noticed sections of the book had been blacked out with a magic marker.

"Who the Hell would do this?" he thought aloud.

He put the book under his arm, intending to alert one of the librarians. Spotting Catcher in the Rye, he flipped through. There were more redactions.

Slaughterhouse Five, Catch-22 and especially, To Kill a Mockingbird--- They had all been censored by some idiot with a magic marker.

Mondel gathered up the books and rushed to the librarian at the front desk. Wendy Stapleton had been working at the library for almost as long as he had been teaching. He just couldn't believe she'd allow something like this to happen.

"Wendy," he gestured, calling her over. "You're not going to believe this."

Wendy, a diminutive Filipino woman with a sweater and short bob cut with streaks of gray, flipped through the books.

"Oh, my God!" she said at normal volume. "Where did--- Are these **our** books?"

"Yeah, I was upstairs talking to a student, just flipping through when I noticed them," explained Mondel.

"Oh, this is a travesty!" she said. "Thank God these aren't first editions or anything. Do you have any idea who would do this?"

As Wendy talked, Mondel spied a student librarian assistant watching them. He had a very guilty look on his face.

"You there," Mondel suddenly said. "Did you know about this?"

The student fled in a panic, heading for an emergency exit. The doctor chased after him. For an academic like Mondel, this vandalism was the ultimate outrage. Charging past the check out desk, he rushed through the emergency exit after him. Outside, he saw the student fleeing across a parking lot and up a hill.

"Wait!" shouted Mondel.

Fortunately, the doctor remembered a short cut through the landscaped bushes he used to use as a student. Back in the day, it was a place to smoke pot on the sly outside. The maintenance guys had mostly gotten the plants to grow back over it by blocking the path with rocks, but it was still there. Mondel hopped over the rocks and took the short cut. On the other side of the path, he caught up with the student. Hopping over the rocks at the other end, he stumbled into him and nearly pushed him to the ground.

"Please!" he begged. "Don't hurt me! She made me!"

"Hurt you?" said Mondel, huffing and puffing. "I'm not going to hurt you. And who made you? Who are you talking about?"

"My girlfriend," confessed the student assistant, sounding despondent. "At least, I think she's my girlfriend, I don't even know anymore!"

"Why the Hell would you deface the library books?" asked Mondel, completely flabbergasted.

"G says the language is problematic, so my girlfriend made me," he whined.

"Listen to me," growled Mondel. "You can't live this way! You have to be a man! You have to stand up for yourself!"

"B-but isn't that toxic masculinity?" he asked sheepishly. "That's what G says."

"Look," said Mondel. "And I'm speaking as one man to another--- She is **not** your girlfriend, do you understand? She's using you to commit an act of vandalism which is unacceptable. You will pay for those books, okay?"

"Can I still let the others in to censor the books?" he asked.

"No! Are you stupid? Of course not!" snapped Mondel. "What is wrong with you?"

"I'm sorry, it's just that my girlfriend is going to be so mad..."

"She's **not** your girlfriend!"

Mondel noticed a book in his hand and a magic marker.

"Give me that," he ordered.

The student put it in his hand and walked away. Mondel looked at the book. It was My Life, the memoir of Golda Meir. He had outlined a quote which he had prepared to black out. It said, "One cannot and must not try to erase the past merely because it does not fit the present."

"Too true, Golda," thought Mondel. "Too true."

The doctor knew it wouldn't stop with just one assistant. The library was incredibly vulnerable. Something had to be done or these people would be censoring the campus Internet next! Regardless of what it cost him professionally or what Professor P might think, he had to go straight to the Dean on this. He had to convince him of the seriousness of the situation before it got really out of hand.

With great purpose, he dialed the phone and started walking.

"What now?" greeted the professor, sounding annoyed.

"They're censoring the books in the library, I'm going to talk to the Dean," Mondel said decisively.

"Jesus Christ," he muttered. "Well, you sound determined. Anything I can say that would stop you?"

"No."

"Well, good luck then."

Chapter 15

Tabitha was in the adjunct professor office getting instructions from Professor Franklin for his updated syllabus. Unlike other adjuncts, she had a higher level of professional fashion sense. She wore a dark maroon blouse with black pants and riding style boots pulled up on the outside. Franklin, as always, was mumbling his instructions.

"I'm sorry, say again?" Tabitha asked.

"Make sure you put The Communist Manifesto in bold," he instructed. "If the students buy only one book, I want it to be that."

"Sure," agreed Tabitha, not really seeing the need.

Madeline, a junior who was a Political Economy, Global Studies and Environmental Justice major, knocked at the doorway. Tabitha gestured for her to give them another minute. Professor Franklin mumbled something about getting the updated syllabi by the next day and headed out. Madeline waited for him to leave before she spoke.

Dressed in a Misfits t-shirt, a black faux-leather jacket and a pair of jeans that were one size too small, Madeline relaxed and addressed Tabitha more casually.

"Hey gal," she smiled knowingly. "We just totally scored a victory. They've rewritten the Spring play the **right** way."

Tabitha looked up curiously. "M. Butterfly? Why would you rewrite that?"

"Uh, because it's problematic?" she retorted, her voice trailing upwards. "We're not going to let the college dictate **our** play."

"Um, well, okay," Tabitha responded. "That seems counter productive."

"It wasn't a big deal. They rewrote it in, like, 30 minutes! No big deal. Plus we've already recast, struck the set and are building a better one. This is going to be **ah-mazing**!" Madeline proclaimed, exhaling in satisfaction.

Tabitha continued to go over her work, waiting for her to get to the point.

"You haven't been to the meetings," noted Madeline. "You know we're the Collective now, right?"

"I've been busy. Did you need something?" Tabitha asked flatly.

"You were active in the old group. We need you in the **new** group," she insisted. "You're currently the only trans professor on campus."

"I'm an adjunct professor. I update syllabi, grade papers and do the legwork around here," Tabitha explained. "Not sure I can help."

"G wants the Collective to have a trans liaison," the junior outlined gauging Tabitha's reaction. "Now I would do it, but I'm not a member of the faculty. Your status will help sell it to the cis-normative types."

Sighing, Tabitha put down her pen and sat back in her chair.

"I appreciate that, but I honestly don't want the drama," declined the adjunct.

"Hmph," Madeline said snidely crossing her arms. "Ya know, you can't hide behind the college forever. They'll come after you too."

"What?" asked Tabitha incredulous.

"You think you can survive in this faculty as the token trans?" scoffed Madeline.

"For the record, I **never** used my status to get this position," Tabitha said a little insulted. "And frankly, adjunct professor isn't exactly **dean**, Madeline."

"Exactly! They put you in here! Make you grade papers! It's like you're their **slave**!"

"It's a **job**. One I worked for," countered Tabitha. "And I remember the days when my status **did** hurt me."

"And you're just going to let them get away with it," said Madeline shaking her head. "If I were you, I'd take a club to their skulls!"

"Madeline," the professor said scolding her. "This is too much."

The junior got a dark look on her face and she took a step back.

"I always knew there was something wrong about you," she said accusatory. "Did you even **get** the operation?"

"I'm not going to answer that," Tabitha bristled.

"You deleted your Twitter account, you date random guys, you don't even hang out with us--- What makes you so trannier than thou?!"

"Madeline, this is exhausting," sighed Tabitha. "I never wanted being trans to define me. I **cherish** the days I don't have to think about this shit. I just want a job and a life--- I wanna write book--- Maybe raise a family. I just want to be **normal**."

"Well, **good** for you," she sneered.

"I have to get back to work."

"Fine. You know what Tabitha? You're on your own now."

Madeline turned on her heel and walked out of the office. The door shut and Tabitha continued to work for a moment. After a minute, she tossed aside the pen again. What was she doing here?

"I hate this job, I hate this drama," Tabitha thought. "And I haven't written page one. I should move back in with my folks. I could save and write the book."

Tabitha turned in her resignation the next day and left Upstate.

Chapter 16

It took a bit of negotiating on the phone, but the Dean agreed to see him. As he drove out of the college, Mondel spotted student protesters at the campus entrance. They were holding signs that said, "No Trump Supporters" and "No Hate on Campus". There was a truck coming to replace the water cooler water and they had stopped him and started yelling at the driver. Mondel pulled over.

"Hey, what are you doing?" Mondel demanded.

"No hate on campus!" one of the protesters immediately said.

"I'm just here to deliver water," said the driver.

"He won't tell us who he voted for!" said one of the Antifa members challenging him.

"Let him through!" Mondel yelled. "He's just delivering water! His politics don't matter! Let him through or I'm calling Safety and Security!"

Despite the breakdown in institutions on campus, this threat still held some weight. The students began to reconsider. The driver prepared to go inside.

"Hey! He's the fascism guy!" recognized one of the protesters.

The undergrads immediately headed for Mondel's car. Scared, he rolled up his window and drove away with the students screaming after him and throwing empty water bottles. As he moved down the hill, he could see in the rear view the water truck driver give up and leave campus.

Pulling up to the gates of the Dean's Residence, he buzzed the p.a. system. The gate moved aside and Mondel drove in and parked. The doctor was now more determined than ever to make Albert understand.

He found the Dean in his living room going over swaths of fabric. His Shih Tzu was sitting on an ornate chair on a handmade pillow that was just for the dog.

80

"Ah, Lawrence, please, come in," smiled the Dean. "Would you like some tea? Something stronger?"

"No, thanks. I appreciate you seeing me, sir," Mondel greeted.

"Which color do you like?" he asked, showing him the swaths. "I'm picking a fabric for a new sash. Have to get this one in for graduation."

"That one," Mondel quickly said, just picking one.

"Really?" the Dean said, surprised. "Oh. Now I don't know what to pick."

"Have you been to campus recently, sir?" Mondel asked.

"No, I've been so busy," he explained. "You know, everyone thinks the Dean's job is easy but I'm under constant pressure to get money, get money. If I'm not begging for donations, I'm supervising the expansion that the donations paid for. You should see the plans for the outdoor amphitheater."

"Does the college need an outdoor amphitheater, sir?"

"Of course!" the Dean said. "We can host outside concerts, outside plays--- Maybe even outside lectures! Granted it will be at the mercy of the weather, which is very dreary here sometimes. But in the summer we should be able to rent the venue. It should pay for itself! I would love to see another production of Othello in a space like that. So much better when Shakespeare is done outside in the elements!"

"Sir, as I said on the phone, this is rather urgent," Mondel explained, trying to focus him.

"I know, you're worried about the protests and what they're saying about you online," he predicted. "Let me say, the college supports you 100%. You're entitled to your political views. If you want to bring a white nationalist to campus…"

"He **wasn't** a white nationalist," Mondel said, carefully trying not to snap at him.

"Hey, I'm as liberal as the next fellow," the Dean assured. "Let the students see those hateful people for who they are!"

"Sir, the students have been protesting non-stop…"

"Good! I love an active student body! They're engaged in politics," he smiled. "That's you doing your job."

"No," Mondel admitted. "On that, I am failure. Look."

Mondel set out some of the books from the library that had been censored. The Dean looked at him curiously and then picked up one of the tomes. He flipped through, noticed the redactions and then flipped through the others. A look of realization came over his face.

"Proust? They censored Proust?" he said, absolutely stunned. "I love Proust. What sort of barbarian would do this?"

81

"The protesting students. The campus is out of control, sir," Mondel said grimly. "You need to do something to restore order."

The Dean suddenly looked very tired. It was like the wind had gone out of his sails.

"The Board of Regents will not be happy about this," he said. "What would I tell the alumni?"

"The truth. The students got out of hand," Mondel counseled. "But if you restore the campus to what it was, they will forget by the time graduation rolls around."

"Do we know the students responsible?" he asked.

"They call themselves G."

"What?"

"The student's name is G, she's insisting on being called they," Mondel said, flustered that he had attempted to follow her gendered pronouns. "The LGBTQ Community and their allies."

"The gay students?" the Dean said, utterly shocked. "But we have gay instructors all throughout the faculty. We support their clubs and their events. We fly the pride flag!"

"It's not just about the gay students, sir," Mondel tried to explain. "There's an ideological component to this that goes much deeper."

The Dean sat back on his couch flipping through the redacted Proust book.

"Did you protest things when you were in college, Lawrence?"

"I think I went to a pro-choice rally once. Protested the Gulf War," Mondel recalled. "You?"

"I went to rallies and marched against nuclear power," he remembered wistfully. "Our professors were always telling us that was the way to do things. That you could change the world."

"Mine too," Mondel agreed. "It's like, if you weren't protesting you weren't a serious intellectual."

"And then you become an academic and you stop protesting. You don't change anything," the Dean said. "You get out in the real world and find out what it's really like out here. It's messy and crazy and unfair."

"Maybe that's what we should be teaching," offered Mondel.

"No one would pay for that," the Dean concluded. "No parent is going to drop $40K a year for us to tell their precious treasure they're not special or that they're probably going to end up as a soccer mom or working at a pesticide company answering phones."

"Do we deserve this?" asked Mondel. "Did we lie to them?"

"To them or ourselves?" shrugged the Dean. "But it is, what it is."

Chapter 17

Since the somber atmosphere on campus had lingered for a long period of time, a group of fraternities took it upon themselves to lighten the mood. Greek Life had always been a footnote at Upstate. They were little more than organizations designed to network, pad a resume and create pre-determined roommates.

Alpha Alpha Alpha led the charge. The frat had a huge house at the neighboring campus on Reid College, an institution that was easily three times the size of Upstate. It had a street of frat houses, some of which had been shut down and gotten in trouble over the years. As an extension of the main Alpha, the Upstate frat felt obligated to organize the party even though their frat house was little more than a glorified dorm.

Chad Amhearst, the president, had gotten the other frats and sororities to contribute and participate. Chad was known as Chad the Chad. He had classically handsome good looks and a muscular physique.

Delta Delta Chi, Omega Pi Nu and Lambda Sigma Rho brought their money, beer pong tables, red cups and girls. Most of the girls were from sororities: Omicron Pi Alpha, Sigma Thi and Kappa Rho. The frats, naturally, had a lot of interaction with them and most sorority girls were dating or had just dated one of the frat brothers.

The bros were strict about carding. They wouldn't get flagged again for underage drinking like they had two years ago. The beer was an IPA called Ms. Stout, a brew aimed at the female market that had been rebranded by Mister Stout BeerCo. Normally, the bros would've bought the regular brand, but it was discounted for female customers in a corporate attempt to pander to a new demo.

Hannah had gone on the trip to the beverage center to save the frat money. The pink kegs had been put in the snow to keep cold and cordoned off with caution tape. Senior brothers supervised everything so that if you wanted to drink, you had to stay inside the area.

New women were monitored closely at the parties. There was an unofficial rule that these girls had a "three drink maximum". The bros found ways not to serve them any more alcohol unless they already knew them and even then, they were wary. Chad and his bros were determined not to get taken down like so many other chapters of their frat.

"Baby, what's wrong?" asked his girlfriend Hannah, draping herself on his shoulders. "Everything's going great."

Chad had an uneasy feeling about the party. The beer pong event was proceeding to cheers and hoots. People were dancing and smiling, but Chad couldn't shake his uneasiness. Perhaps it was something in the air. Hannah was, of course, dressed to the nines in a snow bunny outfit with a fur hat, matching boots and skin tight leggings.

"Ah, it's just weird," he said. "With the student government shut down we couldn't ask for a permit for this thing. Guess we'll just have to pretend it's a spontaneous gathering if S&S shows up."

"Those guys couldn't even stop the protesters, I don't think they're going to come all the way up here just to shut this down," she dismissed. "Besides, the protesters are such dreary bitches!"

"Damn Han'!" laughed Chad.

"It's true!" she insisted gesturing with her red cup. "They all sit around, crying that they hate men and then wonder why no one wants to date them! Uh, hello! Get on a Nordic track and put on some fucking makeup! No one's forcing you to cry into that pint of Ben & Jerry's!"

"Yeah, I know, but there's too many guys," Chad complained. "There hasn't been a real party on this campus for weeks. Normally, you put out some beer and the girls come."

"I know this girl wants to **come**," Hannah said devilishly, sidling up to him.

As the two got cozy in the middle of the quad, they became aware of a noise slowly getting louder.

"Two-four-six-eight! We don't want your fascist hate! Two-four-six-eight! We don't want your fascist hate!"

"Jesus Christ," muttered Chad, turning and seeing the mob.

"Are you fucking kidding me?" Hannah said outraged.

Hannah was prepared to march over and tell G and her crew to fuck off. Chad held her by the arm and calmed her down.

"Whoa-whoa-whoa, babe," said Chad. "We need to be cool. I got this."

The party slowed to a halt as everyone turned toward the protesters. Chad walked out to meet them. He held his arms open as a sign he wasn't a threat.

"Hey, guys," he greeted. "What's up?"

G, Penny and her crew were flanked by Chloe and another trans athlete plus several Antifa members. They had tons of flags and signs addressing everything from U.S. imperialism to housing as a human right. Chad was just kind of hoping they'd leave.

"We are here to protest your exclusionary hetero normative event!" shouted Penny, more for the mob than to answer Chad. "Frats are patriarchal and exclusionary!"

"Uh, yeah, but so are sororities," Chad pointed out. "And the sisters are here."

"You're excluding marginalized people!" shouted Chloe pointing to the caution tape. "What do you call that?"

"The college makes us card people for beer," Chad said incredulous. "They shut us down two years ago over that."

"We're not gonna let you roofie some girl and rape her, you **Chad**!" shouted an Antifa member.

The bros started to get antsy. Chad could hear them saying, "Fuck off." under their breath. He gestured for them to give him another moment, this wasn't over.

"First off, you dumb ass," said Chad bristling. "My name is **actually** Chad. Second, no one is drugging or raping anyone. And third, this isn't a Greek only party. You guys are welcome to join us, if you're cool."

"**If** we're cool," repeated G.

"Yeah, if you're cool," shrugged Chad.

"So **if** we subscribe to your cis normative lifestyle and **if** we cater to your patriarchal idea of gender," G interpreted.

"What the fuck are you talking about?" Chad said, as G ranted.

"And **if** we lay down and spread our **legs** for you! And **if** we worship your literal and metaphorical phallus, while this institution continues to marginalize people of color!" G proclaimed to cheers from the mob.

"Bitch," said one of the black brothers of Omega Phi Nu. "You got more white people in your group than we do! Your crew look like an open bag of marshmallows!"

The brothers burst out laughing. Tyler Brown, who had been standing next to him, laughed uproariously and high fived him.

"See! See?!" raged Penny, pointing at them. "This is the misogyny! This is the hate!"

"We just invited you in!" Chad repeated. "If you don't want to party, why did you come to college?"

"Why do you support fascism and hate?" G asked self-righteously.

"We don't hate people, we're just trying to have a good time and joke around," offered Chad gesturing to the party with his hands. "Can you not take a joke, Ru Paul?"

The brothers laughed again, although not as loudly as the first time. For a second, it looked as if the group might break. Maybe this was all a joke and just like the bros and sisters, they could all party together and forget their troubles. However, one of the Antifa guys picked up an empty bottle and winged it over the mob. It shattered across the head of Chad, causing him to yelp in pain. Blood poured out of his face and he turned away, temporarily blinded by the glass shards and beer.

"Ah, fuck!" he shouted.

The bros surged forward and the fight was on. Hannah, furious that they had attacked her man, spent much of the fight placing her designer boot into the balls of every Antifa member she could find. Chloe punched her so hard, she saw stars. It took four of the bros to take down the muscular athlete.

Some of the party attendees joined the mob. There were too many guys at the event and much of the girl population had joined the protest. By switching sides, they hoped to score some points with the woke girls. The frat's beer pong tables were destroyed. One particularly agile student, climbed up the front of the dorm and pulled down one of the frat's Greek letters. The metal decoration landed on two girls who were standing there watching the fight.

Safety and Security was eventually called, but by they time they arrived on the scene it was mostly aftermath. Every ambulance in town had to make the trek up the hill and several students on both sides ended up in the campus infirmary. Scuffles broke out there as well, as the attackers recognized each other. The final total was one dislocated jaw, three lost teeth, one cracked eye socket, a broken arm, two broken wrists, several broken fingers and black eyes, plus innumerable cuts and bruises.

The riot was on the local news and then mentioned in the national news. Dozens of YouTube videos featuring the fight were played all over Twitter, Instagram, Reddit, Facebook, YouTube, Bitchute, Gab and many other platforms. The details changed with every news report, but one narrative stayed the same: A group of racist frat brothers attacked an LGBTQ event at Upstate College.

The Dean called an emergency meeting of all the department heads that night. Mondel's presence was requested as well. From the Dean's position, Mondel had predicted it and he had the best perspective on the situation. The

Dean was determined to brainstorm a solution by the next morning so they could get on top of the narrative by the end of the next day.

Chapter 18

"What did you say to him?" Professor P demanded, getting into Mondel's car to drive to the Dean.

"The truth!" the doctor said, steering with haste out of the parking lot. "I told him the students were out of control. I told him he had to do something immediately!"

"Goddammit, the optics on this," muttered P.

"I talked to one of my students. The frat boys weren't at fault," Mondel explained.

"It doesn't fucking matter whose at fault!" snapped the professor. "Do you think Albert can lower the hammer on a bunch of queers in this day and age and leave the frat boys alone?! This fuckin' kid, G. I hope one of those drunk idiots punched her clock at least."

"I'm sorry, Professor," Mondel said, not knowing what else to say.

"Stop apologizing," he sneered. "These fucking kids--- You apologize, it's just a sign of weakness to them! When they smell blood, they pounce! Oh! If I were a student now! If I was fifty years younger! I'd call up one of my lesbian beards to smack some sense into her!"

"Jesus, P," Mondel replied a little shocked.

"People think just because you're gay you don't mix it up," laughed P. "We got in plenty of fights and not just with the straights. These kids know it. They're no different! You've probably seen two guys fight over a girl, but you ever see two lesbians? It's the most vicious spectacle you'll ever see! Nails, teeth--- Clumps of hair pulled out. People forget in the fight for equality that we are already equal. We are already the same. We're all shitbags."

"This is getting dark," Mondel said exhaling. "There's got to be some way we can come back from this."

"No, not these people," Papadopoulos assured. "They're radicals. Extremists. Martyrs to a cause with mommy and daddy's credit card to back them."

"Why do we have such little power over them? We're supposed to be the teachers," Mondel thought aloud.

"Because we kept lowering the standards to make more money. College used to guarantee you a job, a career--- Now the only thing it guarantees is a lifetime of debt to a bank and a piece of paper that says you have a four year degree in 'Fabric Arts'," said the professor, disgusted. "Do you want to do something to these people, Lawrence? Do you really want to get back at them?"

"Yeah, I kinda do."

"If either one of those vicious cunts is still enrolled in this institution next year, I want you to promise me to fail them! No matter what the personal costs, the lies you have to tell--- They don't get a degree!"

"There's no way the Dean's going to let them stay here. Right?" asked the worried Mondel.

Professor P sighed. He knew what was coming next.

"Thank you all for making time this evening. I know you all have busy schedules," greeted the Dean in a comfortable smoking jacket and silk pajamas.

Mondel sat next to Papadopoulos. The other department heads: Science, Sociology, Theater, Arts, History and a few others were spread out in chairs across the room. The Dean's dog still had a seat on the handmade pillow.

"First, I'd like to thank Dr. Mondel," said the Dean, pointing him out.

Mondel got very uncomfortable. His body language was screaming, "Please don't draw attention to me."

"He told me some hard truths about the students yesterday and it was tough to hear," he explained. "He tried to warn me of this coming disaster and I just didn't understand the severity. How triggered the students would be when just one Trump supporter comes onto campus."

The heads of the department looked at Mondel. He was squirming in his chair, stopping himself from blurting out the correction. But at least, he had finally arrived at this point. Finally, now would be the reckoning for G and her ilk.

"The fraternities in this country have been on thin ice for years," the Dean said. "It's time I put my foot down."

Mondel was in shock. Was he talking about the frat?

"Two years ago we had an incident and that should've been a wake up call," said the Dean grimly. "As of right now, we will announce there will be an investigation. All frats and sororities on Upstate will be closed until further

89

notice. It's a tough choice. The Board of Regents may not like it, but I'm willing to make that call."

Papadopoulos sighed and looked away. The other department heads applauded the Dean as if he did something brave. Mondel was twisting in his seat and forcing himself not to stand.

"B-b-but sir!" Mondel objected. "What about the protesters? I'm told they started the fight."

"I know, we heard that rumor too," the oblivious Dean said knowingly. "I've already arranged a public meeting with G and her group. Tomorrow morning, I'll meet with them and come to a consensus. The public will be assured and the optics on this ugly incident will be good again."

"Sir, you **can't** do that," Mondel said horrified. "G and her people are not normal students. They won't negotiate!"

"Lawrence, I know you're worried," the Dean said. "Certainly the students have given you the business online."

The Dean held up his phone and played the clip. This time, he turned the sound up as loud as his device would go, "That's fascism!" Mondel heard himself say.

Everyone in the room except Mondel and P chuckled.

"I'm definitely going to say something on your behalf while we're talking to them," the Dean assured.

"We?" Mondel asked, even more horrified. "Oh, no."

"I need you there, Lawrence," the Dean said cheerfully. "You and I used to protest things back in college. We can relate to these kids. Talk at their level."

"No. No, we can't," Mondel begged. "Please sir, these are not some hippie kids that want to smoke pot and listen to the Beatles."

"Albert, he's right," the Professor added, trying to reach him. "If you go into that room without being in a position of strength, those kids will eat you alive. They're taking pages right out of Rules for Radicals, for God's sake."

"Well, I've already accepted their invitation," the Dean informed them. "Seems to me it would be a sign of weakness to back down now."

"**She** invited **you**?" said Mondel, shocked.

"Now-now, she likes to be called they," corrected the dean.

"Where are you meeting her--- They?" asked Mondel.

"The Student Union, of course," the Dean said. "That way, they'll feel more comfortable talking to me and opening up."

"Don't you see, Albert?" the Professor said. "It's a trap! That's just what she wants you to do! She's not going to open up to you! She's going to stab you in the cock!"

Gwendolyn laughed and then stifled herself and cleared her throat.

"Oh, Papadopoulos, don't be so dramatic," she dismissed. "Many of my students are part of the protest."

"What a shock," muttered P under his breath.

"They're just exercising their rights to Freedom of Speech," she assured. "And those frat boys are an awful nuisance sometimes. This way, the Dean takes care of two problems at once."

"With all due respect, Gwen, this isn't a march for equal pay," Papadopoulos corrected. "These kids are acting like hardcore, violent radicals. Makes the Weather Underground, look like the girl scouts! You don't come to a protest in gloves, a bandana and covered in black if you're marching peacefully."

"They're not all dressed like that," she assured.

"Are you marching with them?" Professor P accused.

"Are you?" asked the Dean, very curious.

"I'm not **marching**, I'm just advising and observing," she admitted. "So many of my students are there, I need to keep them engaged in their work somehow. This is all part of being a feminist."

"You're the head of the Art Department," Professor P pointed out. "Not the Gender Studies Department and Karen shouldn't be doing that either. Wait, where is Karen?"

"Karen felt it best to stay with the students," Gwen revealed. "That way, she can be your eyes and ears, Dean."

"Terrific," agreed the Dean, excited at the notion.

"Albert, don't meet them at the Student Union," Professor P tried one last time. "If you're going to meet with her, get her alone and away from the group. You meet her on her own turf, you're as good as dead!"

"I'm sure with everyone's support, it's going to be fine," the Dean smiled confidently. "Besides, this is my college. I rebuilt that Student Union. She can't take that away!"

Chapter 19

Karen Francis, Chair of Gender Studies, was in the campus bookstore calculating how many of her books were still on the shelf. She had assigned *The Patriarchal Capitalistic Complex and the Complicity of (M)Otherhood* to her students in her Masculine Themes in Feminist Literature class. The doctor felt there weren't enough new books being sold and quickly found out why. There were still piles of used copies in the store. They looked new except for the "Used" sticker on the side. Making sure no one was looking, she start to peel off the stickers with her fingernail.

"Dr. Francis?"

Startled, Karen turned. It was Charlene, one of her grad students.

"Oh, hey, Charlene," greeted the doctor.

"I was just at the coffee shop and saw you through the window," said Charlene, a bit frazzled. "I know we talked before, but I thought maybe we could speak in person. You know, maybe set up something during office hours?"

Karen tried not to sigh in exasperation. While Charlene was often a tireless worker under her tutelage, she was like a clingy girlfriend sometimes. The doctor often wanted to cut the cord. This seemed like a good time since Charlene had suddenly grown a backbone. The former Alliance leader was determined to have her say.

"Look, I know it was hard to give up running the Alliance," Karen said. "It was difficult for me too. I helped chaperone the club into existence. But G and the Collective are doing great work here!"

"But all they do is protest and complain," Charlene whined. "I'm not sure what that accomplishes. We seem to be driving away our allies."

"Oh, Charlene," Karen said smugly. "This is a new era. We can't just ask for allies. We have to guide them. We can't just hold a Pride Parade. Using the Internet, we have to bring these people in line."

"In line?" Charlene said, unsure.

"We have to give G as much support as possible," Karen advised. "I can't do it all directly. Sacrifices have to be made."

Charlene suddenly clammed up. She sensed that her mentor's reasoning was heading down a bit of a dark path. The grad student now needed time to process.

"Are we okay here, Charlene?"

"Yes, doctor," she agreed.

In the next aisle of the bookstore, Mandy was perusing the tomes for her major. Consciousness Studies which was mixture of art, psychology and counseling using multicultural analysis. She was taking pictures of the ISBN numbers using her phone on the sly. One of her friends had told her about a website where she could download all the books for free using the number.

Quinn, a junior with homemade tattoos and a septum ring, spotted Mandy. The student looked like a young Gina Gershon dressed in overalls and a fur jacket. Quinn eyed Mandy up and down, liking what they saw.

"Hey, taking pictures?" asked Quinn smiling.

Mandy pulled back her phone, embarrassed she got caught.

"Oh, I was just---"

"It's fine, it's fine," Quinn laughed. "I'm just playing with ya. I'm Quinn."

"Mandy," replied the freshman.

Quinn took her hand and kissed it.

"Enchante," Quinn chuckled.

There was a moment of awkward silence, but not awkward on Quinn's part. Quinn had heard that Mandy had just come out. Freshman girls like that were easy to pick up. Quinn expected to have her back in their room in a couple of hours with her clothes in a pile on the floor.

"Think I saw you at an Alliance meeting---"

"It's the Collective now," said Mandy proudly.

"Cool," Quinn nodded with a grin. "When did you come out?"

"Oh, very recently," said Mandy, adjusting her hair and blushing. "You?"

"Well, you know, some days I feel like a guy and other days, I feel like a girl," Quinn said casually. "It's just like--- I figured that was my thing, y'know?"

93

"How do you feel now?" asked Mandy.

Quinn leaned in close and said intently, "I kinda feel more like an animal now. Like...with some serious urges. You ever get those urges, **Mandy**?"

Mandy could feel Quinn's hot breath on her. Although Mandy enjoyed the attention, the intensity felt too aggressive. The flirty moment had turned into something more ominous.

"I think I should go now," Mandy said, starting to walk away.

Quinn put an arm up against the bookshelf, blocking her way.

"Whoa, c'mon, Mandy," Quinn smiled, trying to laugh it off. "I'm just playin' with ya. I want to get to know you. I think you and I could be really good **friends**."

Quinn went in for a kiss, but Mandy pushed back.

"Hey! No. Seriously?" objected Mandy. "Are you sexually harassing me right in the bookstore?"

"Sexually harassing you?" laughed Quinn. "What are you talking about? I'm not a **guy** right now!"

"I don't like this. This doesn't feel right," Mandy said, looking at Quinn sideways. "Please leave me alone."

"Pfff! Fine, bitch," Quinn dismissed, pretending to look at books, "your pussy ain't made of gold!"

Mandy rushed out of the bookstore. She passed a group of protesters who had come into the shop to look at Bernie Sanders's new book. Sophia was flipping through the pages, reading a chapter on eliminating college debt.

Jeremy was a ginger headed college freshman with mild acne and lanky frame. He had a pile of merchandise in his hands including a sweatshirt, knit cap, mug and shotglass. They all had the Upstate College logo and were pretty overpriced. He also had the Bernie Sanders book, although he didn't really want one. Fortunately, Jeremy still had his dad's credit card, so no biggie.

He was crushing on Sofia, looking over her shoulder. He was desperately trying to think of something smart and woke to say. Olivia was just staring at the cover, imagining what it would be like to make out with Bernie.

"I didn't realize how expensive college **is**!" said Sofia, skimming Bernie's words. "I mean, how are my parents going to **pay** for this?"

"College should be free," Olivia said. "Bernie said it."

"Yeah, he was going to forgive the student debt," Jeremy added. "Guess that's not happening now."

"This is bullshit, Jeremy," Sofia said angrily. "College is a **right** just like healthcare! This school is denying me my rights! It's in the Constitution!"

"Yeah, we shouldn't pay for college--- And we shouldn't pay for these books. This stuff is **ours**. The college owes us."

"Wait, what?" asked Jeremy, not following the train of thought.

"G wouldn't put up with this! This is Capitalism! This is the Patriarchy oppressing us!"

Sofia climbed up on top of the display of Bernie Sanders books and shouted to the rest of the students in the store.

"Hey, everyone!" she proclaimed. "This bookstore is oppressing us! We have a **right** to college! A **right** to knowledge! And a right to these books!"

Sofia grabbed an armful of books and ran out of the store, setting off the theft alarm. The sound blared as the students suddenly started looting the place.

"Whoa! Whoa-whoa! Stop!" begged the manager. "I'm calling Safety and Security!"

Olivia stacked more merchandise on Jeremy's arms as fast as she could. Jeremy's impulse was to stop, but he went along with the pretty girl's demands.

"Go on, Jeremy!" urged Olivia, pushing him through the front door.

As the alarm blared, the Upstate students rushed out of the bookstore with overpriced school supplies, sweaters and giant foam fingers for Upstate's Lacrosse team.

Chapter 20

The next morning, Mondel returned to campus through the back entrance closer to the parking lots. Some of G's protesters were at that entrance too, watching each car that entered. One of the students stood in the road and gestured for Mondel to stop. She was morbidly obese and dressed in an Antifa outfit.

"What are you doing?" asked Mondel.

"Sir, do you belong on this campus?" asked the student.

She was huffing and puffing a little bit. She had been standing up all morning.

"By what authority are you even asking?" Mondel wondered.

"Don't sass me, sir," she said, cradling the short pole to a sign that said "Fascists Get Out!". "We protect this campus."

"Who is **we**? You don't work here, young lady," he pointed out.

The girl smacked his car with the pole.

"I'm gonna ask you one more time," she threatened. "Why are you coming up to this campus?"

"Hey! Don't hit my car!" objected Mondel.

"I'll do what I want, you misgendering scum!" she snapped.

She hit it again and then again. Mondel wasn't sure if he should get out and fight with her or just drive off.

"It's okay. That's Fascism Guy!" one of the other black clad students said. "Let him through."

"You're free to go. For now," she said coyly.

Rather than push the issue, Mondel drove on.

Mondel had arrived at the Student Union an hour early in the faint hope that the Dean had done the same. This way, he had time to talk him out of this

96

terrible plan or at least devise a good escape. The doctor walked passed the basement entrance. It was the most likely place the Dean would have his driver bring him.

Penny, Chloe and the other the trans athlete were sitting on a bench that was used for students waiting for the shuttle. Penny was dressed in a smart business suit, while the athletes wore floral dresses. To Mondel, this was clearly G managing the optics of the meet. Lure the Dean in with seemingly nicely dressed students. Nicely dressed students didn't riot, right?

Instead of going in that entrance, Mondel took an outside staircase up a floor to the quad. Here is where the protest circus was in full swing. The giant pieces of square slate that made up the surface of the quad had all been chalked with giant "G's" and "PBC". Trashcans had been knocked over, flowers had been pulled out and there were papers and debris everywhere.

The Antifa members and LGBTQ members mingled freely, driving any undergrad not with their agenda away from the Student Union. An angry hippie girl was reciting tearful, rage-fueled poetry about the Patriarchy to a group of other girls. They snapped their fingers after the reading and then screamed in unison to the sky. A mannequin dressed like Trump was being ritually stomped on by a circle of protesters. Mondel watched from a distance as two freshmen were blocked by Antifa members on the sidewalk, until they were forced to walk on the grass and away from the Union. This was the protest the Dean needed to see. One of the Antifa members started waving at him.

"Hey, doc! Dr. Mondel!"

"Fawkes?" asked Mondel astonished.

He pulled the young professor away from the throng. He was dressed head to toe in black with a red bandana covered in yellow hammer and sickles.

"Fawkes, what the Hell are you doing?!" Mondel quietly scolded him. "You have to take that off and get out of here!"

"What? You're serious?" he laughed. "C'mon, this is amazing! Look at this place! Have you ever seen anything like it?"

"Yeah, Fawkes, watching the Free Speech Riot in Berkeley on YouTube!" snapped Mondel. "Do you not see what's happening here?"

"Yes! G is putting what you taught her into practice!" he said proudly.

"She dropped out of my class on the second day!" pointed out Mondel. "And she's only a freshman!"

"But they're **protesting**," he said proudly, as if that was all they needed to do.

"Protesting what? She assaulted a speaker! Started a riot! And this protest is tearing the campus apart!" Mondel told him. "This isn't an experiment, it's an incubator for insanity!"

97

"Hey Fawkes!" called a large, broad shouldered woman with half her head shaved. "What did I tell you about talking to other white cis males?"

"Sorry, that's on me," Fawkes immediately deferred. "You're right."

"That's all I wanted to hear," she responded.

"But this is Fascism Guy."

"Don't call me that!" objected Mondel.

"Oh, hey, Fascism Guy," greeted the large woman. "I saw you on Twitter and your video."

For a second, it seemed like she was a fan and not an opponent. Then she lunged aggressively toward Mondel and start yelling at him.

"I don't like Fascists! Get out of our safe space! Now!" she roared. "Can I get some muscle over here?!"

"Oh, you'd better go," agreed Fawkes.

There was an air of hostility. Rather than challenge the authority, Mondel backed away from the quad and went to his office. He poured himself a stiff drink and then texted the Dean.

"Meet me in my office?" Mondel typed. "We can go over strategy."

A few seconds later, he got a reply.

"Too late, we're almost there."

"Fuck!" shouted Mondel.

The doctor stormed out of his office.

"Is everything okay, Dr. Mondel?" asked Dana.

"Dana, whatever happens, no matter what student comes in here, either they have an appointment or they don't get in, okay?"

"Yes, Dr. Mondel."

"Take every precaution, you're not to trust any student without checking with me or Diana," he insisted.

"Yes, doctor, of course," she said worried.

Mondel took a different path back to the Student Union. He rushed up to the basement entrance just as the Dean's car was pulling up. The trans athletes opened the door for him. Out of breath, he stood just behind Chloe as the Dean got out.

"Thank you," said Albert, courteously.

"Dean, we'd like to welcome you to the Post-Binary Collective!" smiled Penny. "It's an honor to have you. Please, take a pamphlet."

"Oh, thank you," said the grateful Dean, pleasantly surprised at the reception.

"Dean, perhaps we could go get a cup of coffee before we start," offered Mondel.

"We have coffee and whatever you need inside," smiled Penny.

"Maybe we can just talk a minute, alone. Dean?" asked Mondel.

"I think we all want to move this forward," Albert said cheerfully. "Come along everyone."

The Dean walked right into the lion's den. Penny made eye contact with Mondel and smiled. It was a knowing smile. Like that of a shark before it bit your face off.

Inside the basement of the Student Union, there was a large room with dozens of chairs and tables. They were filled with scores of young activists. The fight with the frat boys had only increased they's ranks.

Looking around the room, Mondel could see the activist girls, the Antifa boys, LGBTQ Community people and various misfits from the college. There were a few Goths, some hipsters, socialists and Communists. One young man was serving a group of girls bottles of water. They squeezed one in his face, soaking his shirt and laughed at him. He pretended to laugh too, but was clearly emasculated in the process.

In the center of it all, waiting at a table alone was G. Her hair was now every color of the rainbow and she was wearing an old army jacket and a beret. Behind her was a PBC flag and one of her acolytes was already wearing a G T-shirt that was a parody of the famous Che Guevara design. She offered the Dean a chair on the other side. He smiled and sat down. It was lower than her chair.

"Well, this is all very impressive," smiled the Dean. "I like the flag."

"Thank you. Coffee?" said G offering.

"Thank you, yes," accepted the Dean.

"Hello, Dr. Mondel," G said as she poured the cup from a steaming pot that was ready to go.

G acknowledged him, slyly smiling. She had a secret and it was about to come out. Mondel swallowed. He noted a fire exit near by.

"G," began the Dean. "May I ask you what G stands for?"

"G stands for guy, girl, gender, gay," she shrugged. "Whatever I need it to stand for."

"Fascinating," the Dean said with interest. "Look, I know things haven't been easy for students in the LGBTQ Community."

"PBC Community, now," she corrected. "Post-Binary Collective."

"Sorry, my mistake," apologized the Dean.

Mondel winced. The Dean took a sip of coffee. "I know that you and---"

"They," she corrected. "My preferred term is they."

"So sorry," he said again, almost bowing his head in reverence as he did so. "I know that they and them want to get back to class and end this protest."

99

"Hmm, go back to class," considered G, who then turned to the mob. "Do we want to go back to class now?"

"No!" screamed an overweight girl with glasses and a sweatshirt that said "Ask me about my Feminist Agenda". "Keep your hate speech off this campus! Keep your hate speech off this campus!"

"When are you going to stop allowing white cis males to teach hetereonormative stereotypes to unsuspecting freshmen?!" demanded one particularly condescending female student.

"I don't think we do that," the Dean said. "Let's all calm down here---"

"You calm down!" screamed one of the boys, a hipster type who was holding his phone and videotaping the entire event. "When are you going to remove the rape culture from this campus?! How many women have to get **raped** before you do that?!"

With each outburst, the crowd got more and more rowdy. They cheered on the raw emotion and got swept up in it too.

"No one's gotten raped!" the Dean said, feeling cornered, then turning to Mondel. "No one got raped, did they?"

"You don't even **know**!" cried the same student.

"He doesn't even know!" added Santos Ortez-Yama, trying to be part of the mob, pointing with his new bag of soy chips.

A stocky trans man stood, he was shaking with rage. He shoved Santos out of his way. Santos made a surprised noise and fell between a row of chairs.

"Since I transitioned, I can't sleep at night! I lie awake wondering who is going to misgender me and dead name me? Do you know what that feels like?!" he demanded.

"What is that?" asked the Dean, trying to catch up.

"I think you have way bigger problems on this campus, Dean," shrugged G. "But if you resign, we will consider your act of resignation a positive sign towards the community."

"Resign?!" the Dean said, finally getting the memo.

Albert Metuchen stood up, realizing it was fight or flight.

"I am the Dean of this college, young lady!" he erupted.

"They," she corrected.

"Young they! Whoever you are!" sputtered the Dean. "There are rules and regulations on this campus and you will follow them!"

"Oh, so you want to oppress us," said G, throwing up her hands. "What a surprise! The white cis male, who has been having it his way for **thousands** of years---"

"Hasn't been alive that long," muttered Mondel, correcting her.

"Wants the women to go back home and be barefoot and pregnant! Maybe you want to take away our right to abortion while you're at it?! You're as white as Donald Trump! And you think just because your white privilege put you in charge, you can command us?! Well, we're not your slaves, Dean! We will rise up!"

"Yeah!" shouted the room.

"We will be heard!"

"Yeah!" shouted the room.

"We will not be marginalized any more!"

"Yeah!"

"Each one of us is unique!"

"Yeah!"

' "We think for ourselves!"

"Yeah!"

"And we will take what's ours!"

On that last sentence, G threw over the table and the entire room surged toward them. Mondel grabbed the Dean by the lapel and headed for the fire exit. Since he was prepared, he dragged them both through and shut it behind them. It opened to a landscaped area of rocks and Mondel was able to kick a large one over to block the door from opening. The rock was just enough to keep the heavy door from being budged. The students pushed on it from the other side and jammed themselves up against it.

Mondel dragged the Dean around to the parking lot where the car was waiting, but a throng of students had already started rocking it back and forth. They let the Dean's driver escape and he went running down the parking lot as they flipped the car over and cheered.

"C'mon!" Mondel urged the Dean.

The students were going ape shit. They pressed on the fire exit until the entire door and the two glass panels on either side of it shattered. Inside, they were already smashing the place up. Some sort of signal must've went out, because the students that were holding the quad started jumping up and down with glee.

Mondel rushed into some bushes near a dorm and they slipped in the back way to one of the buildings he lived in sophomore year. Rushing through the hallway, they found open doorways and students getting high, playing video games, having sex, drinking beer or doing whatever they wanted. No one seemed to be studying any more. Mondel pulled the Dean into the dorm kitchen and peeked outside the window. The mob of students chasing them moved beyond to the next dorm.

"Okay, I think we lost them," panted Mondel. "You have to call S&S right now."

The Dean was trying to work his phone, but he was having problems.

"Are you okay? What's wrong?" asked Mondel quickly.

"Something wrong with my phone," the Dean said, slurring his words.

Mondel lifted his head up and looked into his eyes. They were dilated.

"Jesus Christ, they drugged you?" said Mondel in disbelief. "I think they dropped tabs of acid in your coffee!"

"Whoa," said the Dean.

Mondel took Albert's phone and dialed Safety and Security.

"Hello?" said the voice.

"We have an emergency," said Mondel breathlessly. "The Dean would like every available S&S officer to get to the Student Union immediately and secure it. We have another riot here."

"Who is this?" asked the voice. "I need the approval of the Dean."

"He's right here," insisted Mondel. "Tell them what's happening. Tell them to go."

"Yes, go!" the Dean managed to say.

"Did you hear that? Please! Hurry!" urged Mondel.

Chapter 21

The call went out to all S&S officers as to what was happening. They had been mildly more prepared since last time. The frat riot was a bit of a blemish on their record and the head of Safety and Security was determined not to let it happen again.

Unfortunately, there was now a fifth column in the department. Two of G's girls had joined S&S as trainees. They were fetching coffee, cleaning up and doing whatever other grunt work the officers needed done. Singularly focused on their work, they had already been rated as some of the best S&S interns security ever had.

But the girls weren't there to help. On this day, they had snuck out and removed every lug nut from all five S&S cruisers in the parking lot. When the officers, two to a car, attempted to drive to campus, they didn't get two feet before the wheels wobbled off and the cars smashed into each other.

Faced with an emergency, the group decided just to take their own cars and deal with the problem later. Unfortunately, they all left their keys in their lockers which were in a locker room. One of the girls had tied the doorknob to another doorknob across the room, making it impossible to open the door.

Back at the dorm kitchen, Mondel was trying to sneak the Dean off campus. They crept through a hallway of open doors.

In one room, a girl with a strap-on dildo was giving instructions to her boyfriend.

"I don't see why I need to get pegged," he complained.

"You have to feel the same pain as me," she insisted. "Now bend over."

In another room, a male was wearing a pair of VR goggles and a device on his bare crotch which was stimulating him. Mondel looked away, wondering why he would leave the door open.

On the other side of the wall, a student was operating the other end of the VR simulator along with a second student. The second student urged him to move a porn star avatar to replicate fellatio.

A group of four girls, sat on the floor of the next room with a Ouija board and several lit candles. They were asking Satan if they could trade their souls for more Patreon patrons.

Through the next doorway, a naked hairy male student in a pig mask was lying on a beach lounge chair. Turning on a tanning light, he started rubbing suntan oil all over his body.

The next room, which was completely empty, was blasting music no one was listening to.

"Where **are** we?" asked the Dean.

"I don't know anymore," whimpered Mondel.

The doctor dragged the Dean out of the dorm of horrors. Using his knowledge of the shortcuts from his student days, he snuck the Dean back to K lot. Albert was looking at his hands. Mondel got him inside his car.

Peering up toward the Student Union in the distance, Mondel could see smoke. He could hear glass breaking and students cheering. It was all like Lord of the Flies writ large. Mondel got in his car and started driving them to the back entrance.

When he reached it, he found the Antifa students had pushed vehicles to block the way and lit them on fire. They were dancing around them in glee waving their protest signs. They said things like "No Hate!", "When You Date a White It's Not All Right" and "All My Heroes Kill Cops".

"Shit!" Mondel said.

"Whose cars are those?" asked the Dean.

"I have no idea," said Mondel, turning around.

The doctor realized that if he didn't make it to the front of the school in time, it's likely the students had it blocked too. They'd be trapped on campus until they could get real cops up to the school. On the way to the front entrance, they passed a group of six S&S officers jogging up to campus. They had gotten fat over the years of sitting in their cruisers, so they looked out of breath and not threatening.

"God speed," sighed Mondel, wishing them the best.

When the officers reached the edge of the parking lot of the Student Union, they could see the chaos. Sgt. Tompkins, the leader, knew already they did not have enough guys to secure the building.

"Fu-uck," said Timmy, one of his officers.

"Suck it up, Timmy," the Sergeant barked. "We got a job to do."

"Yeah, but what do we do, Sarge?" asked Russell, one of the other officers.

"Already got the intel," the Sarge said confidently. "This is all being led by Milkshake Girl. We arrest her, it ends. Cut off the head and the body will die."

Through the side window of the Student Union basement, Sgt. Tompkins could see G preaching to the converted masses.

"Bingo," he said in anticipation. "Just her and we leave immediately."

As the six officers strode forward, a group of female protesters flanked by Chloe and the other trans athlete, carried a large drum full of something heavy. The girls opened the doors of the Student Union to let them out and they tossed the drum forward. A huge wave of foul, red liquid spilled out of the drum and ran down the gradual grade of the parking lot. It went past the shoes of the officers who were suddenly hit by the smell.

"Oh, my God," gasped Timmy.

"Fuck, what is that?" gagged Russell.

"It's the Collective's Menstral Blood!" announced Chloe. "And I contributed!"

Timmy and some of the other officers vomited. They all ran to the side of the parking lot to get away from the smell. The Sarge had had enough.

"I don't get paid enough for this shit," Sgt. Tompkins announced.

Expecting an easy gig corralling drunk college students, the Sergeant could only imagine the nightmare of paperwork if he had to fight his way through a group of LGBTQ students to get at G. He figured it was just easier to find another job. He left, tossing away his hat and tie, never returning to Upstate College again.

Minutes later, a group of Antifa guys, sensing weakness in the remaining officers, started hurling clumps of dirt, rocks and empty latte containers in their direction. The rest of the S&S, completely demoralized, headed back for the office.

At the same time, Mondel was driving cross campus to the front gate. Along the way, he passed more protesters. A group of them were defacing the campus chapel, having painted an enormous "G" on the side and placing the "PBC" flag across the entrance which covered the inscription "All faiths welcomed".

Mondel made it to the front gate, but the students had dragged a cement barrier across one side and a massive tree trunk across the other. They also set the tree on fire for added effect. They were dancing at their victory and didn't see the doctor's car approach. His one chance was to drive around the gate in the grass, the only problem was an enormous ditch he would have to traverse to

105

do this. The doctor figured he had to be going fast enough to go down and up the curve, but not too fast that he'd jump the hill going down and smash into the other side. He also had to go fast enough or he wouldn't make it out of the steep hole.

"Dean, I'm about to try something risky," he announced.

"You should always take risks," the Dean advised. "You're in college."

"Hey," said one of the students noticing. "Is that Fascism Guy?"

Mondel was out of time. He gunned the engine, hit the slope perfectly and cleared the other side! Unfortunately, his little car got to the top and the back bumper caught as he landed. The wheels didn't catch and he flopped over sideways.

"Dean? You okay?" he asked immediately.

"Did we crash?" he said astonished.

"Yes, c'mon," he urged.

Mondel was climbing out of his car. He could see the students rushing down the hill. He wasn't sure what they would do to them as this point, but he wasn't sticking around to find out. The Dean climbed out after him and Mondel pulled him down the hill. The students turned his car back on four wheels and then pushed it into the ditch. They cheered.

Escorting the Dean back to his house, the doctor called the professor as they reached the front gate. The Dean fumbled with his keys trying to remember which one opened it.

"Professor, I think they took the campus," said Mondel out of breath over the phone.

"I know," P replied. "It's all over the national news."

"What? That fast?" said Mondel in shock.

"They were taping everything," he explained. "You almost don't have to tell me what happened. In fact, there are some things I can tell you. Stay out of the Student Union parking lot for a while."

"What are we going to do, Professor?"

"I don't know, Lawrence," Papadopoulos said, searching his mind for the answer. "Tell Albert to call in the real police. Arrest the whole damned school if they have to."

"They drugged the Dean," Mondel revealed, helping Albert find the right key. "He's in no condition to call."

"I have to hand it to that kid," the professor said with mild admiration. "She's got balls as big as Death Stars. All right. I'll call the assistant deans. Maybe they can get things rolling. You okay?"

"They got my car, but other than that," he explained. "Are we fired?"

"Fired? You'll be lucky if there's a college left to be fired from," concluded P. "Hang tight. I'll get back to you."

Chapter 22

For the next six hours, Mondel babysat the Dean. Mostly he just kept asking obvious questions and looking at his hands. Starving, Mondel went right into his kitchen. The Dean's dog followed. Finding the creature's food packs, Mondel gave the little guy his dinner and then helped himself to leftovers from the fridge.

The Dean ate like a French Monarch. His fridge was full of to-go boxes from every high end restaurant in the area, including the Concord. One had a receipt from GrubHub and Mondel noticed the address for the eatery was several miles away. He must've spent a small fortune just on the delivery charge. Mondel made himself a plate, then came back out into the living room to turn on the TV and watch the Dean. He opened a fancy beer for himself.

"Where'd you get that food?" asked the Dean.

"Kitchen," Mondel said.

"Cool," agreed the Dean. "Is there any Veal Ossobuco left?"

"Sorry, no," said Mondel, realizing that's what he was eating.

"Oh, well," he shrugged.

Every major network was covering the riot at Upstate, only that wasn't the narrative. The narrative was, "Miracle at Upstate College" and "Student-Run Protest Attacked" and Mondel's favorite, "LGGBDTTTIQQAAPP+ College Community At Risk". No one at any of the major media companies seemed willing to criticize G. Penny had crafted press releases to all of them "explaining" the events and emailing the appropriate footage. The news stories had different details, but the narratives were exactly the same. They all went something like this:

Tonight! Upstate College and the student protesters facing backlash. We have this report: (It would then cut to a second reporter who would do the voice over, not that they were even on the scene.) What started as a protest for a gay and trans right activists, has spiraled into what some experts are calling…the biggest hate crime in U.S. History. The Post-Binary Collective, a movement of gay, lesbian, people of color, trans and other marginalized groups, has been actively fighting the rise of fascism on the Upstate College campus.

Several weeks ago, when a white supremacist was allowed to recruit in a college class, the group formed to protest. The PBC, led by G, as they are called, was accused of throwing a milkshake at the hate merchant before being immediately arrested by campus police. For the next several weeks, G and her group of activists struggled to make their voices heard. (This was followed by a montage of several heroic stills of G and the protesters and not-so heroic stills of the frat brothers bathed in red.) They faced an out of control fraternity system and an administration that continues to ignore them.

Speculation now centers on this man, Dr. Lawrence Mondel, who originally brought the racist speaker to campus. Why did the college allow Mondel, an alleged doctor of political science, to bring such a divisive and hateful guest to campus? One thing is for sure, authorities are most likely interested in talking to Mondel now that the campus has erupted in anger. (The other anchor would then break in to ask a question.) Will Mondel take responsibility for what he's done? (The other reporter would then say.) We tried to reach Dr. Mondel for a comment, but he did not respond. More on this story as it develops.

After just one of those reports, Mondel found some plastic wrap, covered up the rest of his plate and put it back in the fridge. He couldn't eat now, but he did down the beer. He spent the evening watching the news and drinking a few more fancy brews. Penny was calling into the news stations, explaining how the PBC was attacked and that they were forced to defend themselves. No one at any of the news stations had reporters on campus. Not one of them checked to see if anything Penny was telling them was true.

Finally, his phone buzzed. It was P. Mondel walked to the far end of the room so that the Dean could not hear the conversation.

"Are the town cops coming?" asked Mondel hopefully.

"No," said P.

"What? Why?"

"Because the town hates the college," sighed the Professor. "Remember three years ago when two of our black students were accused of shoplifting in that bakery? Remember the protests that shut it down?"

Mondel recalled. The students eventually confessed to the shoplifting, but the resulting boycott bankrupted the bakery, which had been a town

109

institution for three generations. The doctor was now recalling several instances like that where the over sensitive student body either staged a protest or boycott or sued some business or institution in the town.

"They're not stupid," the Professor said. "They don't want their fingerprints on this. Legally, they're not even obligated to help the campus unless Safety and Security calls them and no one can reach Sgt. Tompkins."

"What about the Assistant Deans? P, they're tearing the campus apart!" cried Mondel. "They have to do something!"

"Those four idiots keep voting on everything and ending it in ties," growled the professor. "Like some retarded Politboro. Is Albert back on his feet yet?"

Mondel turned around. The Dean and his dog were gone.

"Maybe, I'll have to call you back," said the doctor hanging up. "Dean?"

Rushing through the house, Mondel could not help but notice the opulent furnishing, carpets and decorations. The Dean's house was full of antiquities and exquisite pieces of art.

"And tuition keeps going up and up," muttered Mondel to himself.

The doctor moved up a hand carved staircase and stumbled into the Dean's bedroom. He had a four poster bed, a shoe closet and a bathroom with gold plated fixtures. He noticed some of the drawers in the Louis XIV dresser were open and clothes were mostly gone. He looked outside the window and saw the Dean packing his suitcase in his car.

"Hey!" Mondel shouted, causing the Dean to hurry.

Running back downstairs and out the door, he stood in the driveway just as Albert was about to get into his car. His dog was in a carrier on the front passenger seat.

"Where the Hell are you going?!" demanded Mondel.

"Oh, I have plenty of vacation time saved," explained the Dean. "It's in my contract."

"The school is being destroyed!" Mondel shouted in outrage. "You're just going to leave it?!"

"It's **their** school Lawrence! If they want to burn it to the ground, who are we to stop them?" the Dean suggested.

"Are you crazy? There are innocent students up there! They had nothing to do with this! Why aren't you stopping her?!"

"They," corrected the Dean.

"It doesn't matter! Why?!" demanded Mondel.

"Her father is on the Board of Regents," the Dean explained. "He's donated millions over the years. It's his sandbox and his daughter is playing."

"Why would he want her to ruin the school?!" shouted Mondel.

"Because he doesn't think she is!" snapped the Dean. "He's followed the news reports and the social media! He thinks she's involved in a 'grand experiment' to 'change the world'! It's just what **his** college professors told **him** to do! It's what our school tells everyone to do!"

The Dean's words resonated with Mondel. There was no hint of Albert's over confidence or flightiness anymore. He was being real. At heart, he was a money man and always knew the score. This wasn't a college. It was a playground built by the rich for their spoiled spawn.

"My advice, get out of town," advised the Dean. "Find another college to teach."

"But...I-I-I have tenure," Mondel said, his voice quivering.

"Oh. I'm so sorry," the Dean apologized.

Albert got into his car, started it up and drove away from the stunned political science teacher.

Chapter 23

G consolidated her hold on the college. Using her fifth column inside the Safety & Security apparatus, the students successfully drove away the rest of the officers from campus with threats of a hate crime lawsuit. None of the security detail wanted that trouble. They resigned and fled, rather than get tied into something that could bankrupt them. Chloe formed a group and took over S&S with the girls that had assisted during the stand at the Student Union. Additionally, the S&S building was looted for its body armor, batons and other riot gear. It was passed out to the new student officers and Antifa members.

It was the weekend, so the college would have two days before classes would need to start up again. G set up shop inside the Student Union. She made plans to completely rewrite how the college was run, all the while calling into major news networks to give updates on the "struggle" against fascism.

Mondel called Triple A and fortunately, the service was available to him 24/7. He got the tow truck driver to collect him and creep up on the ditch at 3:30 in the morning. The students guarding the front entrance either didn't see the truck or didn't care. The tow truck driver pulled his car out and onto the shoulder of the road. It was banged up, but pretty drivable. The students had spray painted "Fascism Guy" across the driver's side.

"You want me to tow it to my shop? Fix this up?" asked the driver.

"Nah, I think I'll be okay," said Mondel. "But we should hurry, I don't want them to see us."

"What's happening at the college?" he asked.

"It's a long story," sighed Mondel.

"I almost went to college," said the driver. "But I bought this truck and I've been making money ever since. You know how it is. But I always thought about taking a few classes. You know, bettering myself."

"Do you like what you do?" asked Mondel.

112

The driver shrugged, disconnecting Mondel's car and winding up the winch.

"Pays the bills," he said. "I'd like to make more money, but who wouldn't right?"

"You do something good. You do something real," noted Mondel. "You help people."

"You're a college professor!" laughed the driver. "You helped lots of people, I'm sure!"

Mondel glanced up the hill. One of the Antifa guys set off some fireworks. The bottle rocket hit a tree and exploded. He and the other students cackled like hyenas.

"Yeah," Mondel said, flatly, getting into the car. "I used to think so."

He started it up and the engine sounded fine. One of the headlights was out.

"If you get stuck, your policy won't cover another visit for free for twenty-fours. Just call a friend to get a ride and wait, then I'll come back. Okay?" advised the driver.

"Call a friend," Mondel repeated, suddenly getting an idea. "Yes, thank you!"

Mondel gave his electronic signature to the driver and headed out. He rushed back to his apartment. There was no time to waste. His former college roommate was a big shot editor at the Press of New York, one of the largest media companies on the East Coast. Now that this was in the national arena, he could call Jared and get him to fight the narrative.

Back at the apartment, Mondel dialed.

"Hello?" said a sleepy voice.

"Jared? It's Lawrence, sorry to bother you so late," he apologized. "But it's an emergency."

"Hey, buddy, great to hear from you," he said groggily. "Hold on, let me get out of the bedroom."

Jared walked to a different part of his house so he wouldn't wake his wife. He poured himself a glass of water in the kitchen.

"Something wrong? What happened?" he asked.

"Did you not hear what's been happening at Upstate?" the doctor asked.

"To be honest, I was at an award ceremony when the story broke," he explained. "I was actually going to call you tomorrow to get the deets. The editorial board wasn't sure it was all that newsworthy for a story."

"Jared, you have to send a reporter right now!" insisted Mondel. "The entire college is being destroyed by political radicals!"

113

"Whoa-whoa, calm down," he said. "Is this some kind of Trump supporter thing? Bunch of red caps bothering the students?"

"No, it's nothing like that!" Mondel dismissed. "It's a fifth column! My own students they've--- They've turned into extremists!"

"Right, who support Trump," said Jared understanding.

"No! They're Neo-Marxists!" Mondel explained. "The leader, G, hit the speaker with a milkshake. We tried to discipline her, but she's refused to listen to the student government, the administration--- It's like the riot during the Inauguration in 2016! They have guys dressed as Antifa running around!"

"Jesus," gasped Jared. "And they're fighting the fascists?"

"There are no fascists! It's a college campus! You've been there! No one there is a fascist!" yelled Mondel.

"All right, Lawrence, all right," said Jared. "We'll get to the bottom of this. You have to give me a statement though, **on the record**."

"Absolutely," promised Mondel. "I'll do all the interviews you want, but you have to get the truth out!"

"The truth always comes out, my friend," assured Jared. "Trust me. I'll put one of my best guys on it."

"Thank you so much, Jared!" Mondel said in relief. "You just don't know how it's been the past few weeks. I've been a wreck! It's worst than the divorce."

"Buddy, you just let me take care of it, okay?" he assured. "Touch base soon."

Mondel hung up. He felt like a huge weight had been lifted from him. Then he went into his broom closet and found a can of old spray paint he had used to paint some lawn furniture. He didn't want the neighbors to see what was written on his car, so he covered it up with the can as best he could.

Watching the paint drip down the side of his car and onto the street, he felt a sense of control return. This had been a perfect storm for G and she may have defeated the college system--- If only because of her parents--- But surely, her ideology could not stand up to the withering glare of sunlight. The Press of New York would expose her for the fraud she was.

Mondel went back inside, stripped off his clothes and fell onto bed. He imagined a future in which he gave talks on the events of Upstate. There was definitely a book in it. He could called it "College Out of Control" or something. It would be a damning treatise of the corruption of the collegiate system. There would be change. Upstate would survive this. He would survive this.

The doctor drifted to sleep with these happy thoughts.

Chapter 24

Tyler had gone to the Campus Pub to draw the building before it was torn down. Back in the day, when the drinking age was 19 in New York, it had been a student bar. But after the age went to 21 in the late 80's, it went into a slow decline from which it never recovered.

Through much of the 90's and 2000's, it had become the college's defacto venue for stand up comics. But by the 2010's, the comedians stopped coming and the college made the decision to tear it down next year to build a cultural heritage museum.

The sad decay of the old comedy club appealed to Tyler's artistic sensibilities. He wanted to capture the faded flyers that still hung in the display case near the entrance. It advertised prop comics and an open mic night. Someone had plastered a "Stop the Hate" sticker across the top of the glass.

As Tyler sketched the snow covered steps of the pub from the nearby stone park bench, he shifted his weight. He wasn't sure how much longer he could stand the cold on his ass.

"Ty! Ty!"

Tyler looked up. It was Greg and Billy walking over from the upper classman dorms.

"You're drawing this dump?" asked Greg.

"Gotta draw something," shrugged Tyler. "Where are you two coming from?"

"Upper classman dorms," said Greg. "It's fuckin' lit there, bro!"

"It is crazy insanity!" Billy agreed. "There was a naked guy in a pig mask sunning himself on a balcony!"

"Nothing's crazier than what happened at the Student Union, I hear," said Tyler bemused.

"Fuck all that," Greg said explaining. "Everyone knows Safety and Security ain't doin' shit right now! Everyone over there is getting drunk and high---"

"And you can buy a blowjob for $50!" laughed Billy.

"What the fuck?" said Tyler, mildly horrified.

"One of the senior girls broke up with her boyfriend and she's letting anyone else with a dick unload as revenge!" Greg said gesturing with his hand like he had found paradise.

"But you have to bring your own condom," added Billy.

"Of course," agreed Greg. "We're not animals."

"What the fuck is happening on this campus?" asked Tyler, not liking the implications.

"Are you kidding? It's finally gotten cool!" surmised Greg.

"I am starving!" said Billy. "Let's hit a dining hall."

Tyler walked with the duo as they drifted across the campus.

"Can't go to the one near the Student Union right now," Tyler reported. "Let's head up to the big one."

"Yeah, I can eat," Greg agreed. "Let's take the access road. It'll be faster."

Making their way up the access road that the maintenance guys used for their vehicles on campus, the trio headed for the main dining hall. As Tyler walked, he saw something out of the corner of his eye. They were passing by two of the other dorms. Most of the lime green buildings were surrounded by trees and shrubs almost all the way around. From their vantage point on the roadway, Tyler could see someone at an outside window.

"Holy fuck," exclaimed Tyler.

The other guys turned. Santos Ortez-Yama had perched himself on a tree to peer into the second story window of the girl's shower and was jerking it to whatever he was looking at.

"Hey! You jerk off!" shouted Greg. "Not cool!"

Santos lost his balance and fell into the bushes as a girl inside the window screamed. The guys quickly slid down the hill to confront the wanker. He was desperately trying to pull up his pants when they found him.

"What the Hell is wrong with you, Santos?" said Tyler, disgusted with him.

"I was just--- I fell and my pants came down," Santos stammered, finally getting his jeans up.

"Should we call Safety and Security?" asked Billy.

"They're not gonna come," scoffed Greg.

"Just like Santos," joked Tyler.

116

Greg grabbed the overweight college student as he tried to push his way out of the bushes.

"Guess we do this Old School," said Greg, winding up to punch him.

"Stop!" insisted Mia.

Mia, along with several girls in their bathrobes and slippers, had rushed out to see what the commotion was all about it. Greg looked at them, incredulous.

"We don't need to be white knighted, thank you," sneered Mia, folding her arms.

"He was jerking off while looking at you through the window!" said Greg, astonished that these girls would defend him.

"It's my toxic masculinity!" insisted Santos. "I'm really trying to deal with it! I'm a struggling feminist!"

"You see?" said Mia. "He's just as much of a victim."

"What?" said Greg, almost unable to process what he was hearing.

Santos started crying, "I'm sorry! I'm so sorry!" he sobbed.

Greg let him go. He, Tyler and Billy started backing away from the scene as the girls assured Santos that he was forgiven.

"The fuck just happened?!" asked Greg as they walked back up the hill.

"That was even crazier than what was happening in the upper classman dorms," noted Billy. "Only not as fun."

"This place is **not** worth a student loan," added Tyler.

Chapter 25

When Paul Freidman got the assignment from Jared, he knew it was a perfect story for him. Freidman, a Harvard graduate, had previously majored in Gender Studies before switching to Journalism. The tall, skinny, bespectacled reporter had interned at Populi.com and worked for The Agenda for a year. Both were hard left leaning news sites that weren't afraid to expose the racism and homophobia inherent in the system. He was already sure that G had done this to her college.

Freidman arrived in the dining hall parking lot. He was greeted by the smartly dressed Penny, who shook his hand and guided him inside.

"Thank you so much for coming, Mr. Freidman," she greeted. "If you'll walk this way, G is waiting."

"Thank you," Freidman said, enjoying the show of respect.

Freidman was only 26 and Penny was very pretty. Such deference was not given to him at the Press of New York, where the other reporters considered him little more than a glorified intern. Two Antifa members walked with Penny, one of them carried Freidman's bag for him.

G had moved her base of operations to the main dining hall. She was running the student government inside the cafeteria in full view of the other students. Standing on either side of her were Chloe and another trans athlete wearing the Safety and Security uniforms. The students were eating in other parts of the cafeteria. It all seemed pretty normal, except that G had a table to herself with various papers and mobile devices spread out on it.

"Mr. Freidman," greeted G. "Thanks so much for coming. Welcome to the Collective. Can I get you a drink? Are you hungry?"

"Water, please," he requested.

Immediately, Chloe put ice in a glass, poured in water and set it in front of him.

"Thank you," smiled Freidman. "Do you have a straw?"

"Straws hurt the environment," said G. "We had them all thrown away."

Friedman seemed impressed by this. He began his interview. "Let me start by asking, what is your preferred pronoun?"

"They," G replied.

This exchange solidified the confidence between the two. Penny sat down next to G on her left.

"And Penny?" asked Freidman.

"Hmm," she wondered aloud. "I'm queer-fluid, but I've been feeling very fem recently. With G's permission, of course, you can call me womxn."

"Well, I'm cis white male," said Freidman embarrassed. "Please don't hate me."

Freidman was joking. The women laughed. G mentioned something like "We'll struggle through it." The smugness was palpable.

"Would you mind if I recorded this?" requested Freidman.

"Oh, don't worry, save your phone," Penny offered. "I'll record the whole thing and send it to you. The wifi here--- We can't give out the password."

"Not even to me?" laughed Freidman.

"The fascist are everywhere," assured G. "It's for your protection."

"Okay," agreed Freidman. "Saves me time. Tell me about how you're fighting fascism here."

Freidman allowed G to launch into a long speech about how the PBC led the brave struggle to break the Patriarchal bonds of the college system. To hear her tell it, her group was beset on all sides by racists, fascists, Republicans, Trump Supporters, homophobes, Neo-Liberals and even Liberals.

Since they had moved into the dining hall, they had liberated the dining hall staff. Many of them were illegal aliens. The students promised them citizenship and increased wages. They paid them out of the student government money, which one of the fifth column members of Chance's administration had gained access.

Much of the maintenance crew had quit, despite the promises of more pay. They didn't feel safe on campus any more after one of them in a red cap was attacked by Antifa members. He wasn't a Trump supporter, he'd just happened to be wearing a red cap.

In order to promote women in STEM fields, G had proclaimed that the maintenance crew be replaced by female students, mostly from the art department. While the girls could build interesting paper machete sculptures and kiln-fired mugs, they knew little about fixing the hot water heaters or plowing the campus parking lots.

119

G presented it all as running smoothly. This was true, insomuch as the people she appointed hadn't had to fix anything yet and the student government money, although rapidly being spent, was still there.

"Interesting," noted Freidman, not bothering to question any of it. "So the Liberals are against your experiment too."

"Boomers," said G knowingly. "But I wouldn't call it an experiment. Experiments are theories that are being tried. What we're doing **works**. We're crafting a new, inclusive society where marginalized people will never again not have their voices heard. Come, let me show you."

G stood using her cane and placing one hand behind her back, walked through the college dining hall pointing out the various groups. Freidman thought they were just students catching a bite or doing homework, but these were G's people. They were doing important work for the Collective.

"This is Karen, the Chair of our Gender Studies Department," introduced G. "This is Paul Freidman from PNY. Tell him what you're working on, Karen."

"Thank you, G," Karen said excitedly. "I'm working with the students here discovering new genders."

"Really? That sounds fascinating," Freidman complimented. "How many new genders have you discovered?"

"Oh, dozens!" she beamed. "But we're going beyond that!"

"Yes," agreed Mandy, one of Penny's first converts to Cause. "Karen is working on a theory of **infinite** genders!"

"I call it Fifth Wave Multi-Dimensional Genderism, it's exciting research," Karen claimed. "I don't think we would've been brave enough to pursue this without the leadership of G, here."

Freidman took it all in as rote without asking a question. In college, he had been considered the laziest of intellectuals. It was why he had to change majors to Journalism. Not even the Gender Studies professors would encourage his tired, derivative arguments. But here, on the campus of Upstate, he was being treated as he should've been treated. He was important, accomplished and about to expose the world to a great thing he was "investigating".

G smiled at Freidman. She liked that easy way he just accepted everything. She guided him to the next planned exhibit. Mel Franklin was sitting at a round cafeteria table with four other students. One had a beret, another was vaping and the other two were sipping cappuccinos. They had stacks of books on slavery in America, Das Kapital by Karl Marx and, of course, The Birth of Biopolitcs by Foucault.

"This is Professor Franklin and some of his young thinkers," G introduced. "They're working on reparations for the campus."

"Reparations?" said Friedman, finally asking a question. "So you're going to give the African-American students their due?"

"Oh, it goes way beyond that!" chuckled the professor. "We're calculating reparations for all victims of slavery--- Going back to the building of the Pyramids of Giza!"

"Astonishing!" exclaimed Friedman. "Can such a calculation be made?"

"It's difficult to perform such a mathematical undertaking," admitted Franklin, "but we've tried to account for race, gender, religion, wars, plagues, patriarchal institutions, workplace accidents, climate change, natural disasters---"

"You must be calculating variables from all of human history!" Friedman said, trying to wrap his brain around it.

"Yes, it's important work," agreed Franklin. "The Egyptian students will be working off quite a debt."

G moved the tour along. Sitting in a circle of beanbag chairs, two female students were leading a group of male students in crying.

"This is our Crying Club," G explained. "It's a place where we help men get in touch with their feelings by making them cry. Males need to get in tune with their feminine side and this facilitates it."

"C'mon! Cry! You call that crying!" screamed one of the girls. "C'mon, you little bitch! You little small dicked bitch! Cry for me! Cry!"

The male students, mostly guys that already supported women's rights, agreed to join the club at the urging of their female friends. They were called "The Cucks" in secret at first, but the name was slowly becoming acceptable to use as time went on. The few that had girlfriends were expected to be in non-monogamous, polyamorous relationships with them. Kyle was amongst the group. He joined the club after Heather threatened to break up with him if he didn't. He was especially good at crying now.

"Wow," said Freidman. "This is--- Wow, mind-blowing! I thought I was a feminist, but I have so much to learn."

"The Collective is going to transform Upstate," G vowed. "Tell your readers that I promise, they won't recognize this place in a few weeks. We're going to achieve true equality for marginalized people. Diversity is a strength and with the amount of diversity we now have at our fingertips, **no one** can stop us."

Freidman spent the next hour being led by the nose exactly to where G wanted him to go. A group of Antifa members stayed ahead of the tour, picking up trash and clearing the quad of anyone that might disrupt it or counter the narrative. At one point during the tour, a student in a pig mask, high on mushrooms ran naked out of a dorm.

121

G laughed and then nodded to Chloe and another trans athlete to take care of it.

"This is still a college," G smiled. "People still have the freedom to do crazy things. He'll be taken care of."

The trans women carried the pig student back to his dorm. But when they got inside, they took him into a shower stall and beat him with their batons.

"Don't do that again!" growled Chloe. "When reporters tour this campus, you don't fuck around, understand?!"

"Hey, c'mon, man," laughed the student.

"Don't misgender me!"

The trans athletes left the pig faced undergrad bruised and bleeding in the shower. Freidman, of course, saw none of this. In fact, Penny had taken the liberty of editing out the incident when she emailed the video footage to him from her phone. She had also cut the clips into nice short sound bytes. Freidman was happy to have his work done for him and thought nothing of it.

Later, Freidman had a sumptuous meal prepared by the dining hall staff and served by some of the Cucks. Amongst the servers was Fawkes.

"Here you are," said Fawkes, handing him his falafel platter. "I hope you enjoy that."

"Paul Freidman, this is Professor Fawkes," G introduced.

"You're serving in the cafeteria?" smiled Freidman, mildly confused.

"Of course!" smiled Fawkes happily. "As a white cis male, it's just part of the way I atone for my gender and race! Now I'm off to clean the kitchen!"

Chapter 26

Mondel stayed away from the campus for the day, as did the rest of the staff. The thinking was to let things cool down until a solution could be reached. The assistant deans were continually deadlocked, but fortunately for them, the parents of the students were under a false impression. Their kids were participating in a grand experiment rather than being held on a campus that was under siege.

The doctor drove down town to buy a replacement headlight and spend his day off relaxing, if that was possible. This thought was short lived, as some of the students dressed as Antifa had also come to town. They spotted Mondel in the parking lot.

"Hey, Fascism Guy!" called one of the students. "You fuckin' dick!"

One of them threw a stick in his direction.

"Hey!" objected Mondel weakly, although secretly he was just glad the stick didn't hit him.

The students headed for the Vegan V which looked overwhelmed with customers. Mondel assumed they were making money hand over fist, but the truth was the students weren't paying. The restaurant was on the verge of collapse.

Mondel walked over to the newspaper vending machine for the Press of New York. The town still had enough old timers that the dispensers were still filled. Upstate was on the cover and he had high hopes "The Paper of Best Record" would correct the story.

"Bold College Embraces Inclusion!" was the headline. Freidman had written a glowing article, tripping over himself to compliment G. He also spent several paragraphs calling the doctor fascist, racist and homophobic, even though the reporter never even contacted him.

"Goddammit, Jared!" Mondel said aloud.

Suddenly, there was the screech of tires. Mondel had been so distracted, he didn't even see the van rolling up to him until it was too late. The door was already opened and two men in black, wearing ski masks, threw a hood over him and pulled him inside. Mondel struggled.

"This is it!" the doctor thought. "They're finally going to kill me!"

"Dr. Mondel! Dr. Mondel!" said one of the kidnappers. "It's me! It's me! It's okay!"

Mondel pulled off his hood. He recognized the voice and then the kid, who had removed his ski mask. It was Conrad Montague, one of his students from his American Constitutional History class.

"Conrad?" said Mondel, stunned. "What are you doing? Why did you kidnap me?"

"We're sorry, we didn't want the Antifa guys to see us talking to you," he explained. "It's for your own protection. We're the Incel Resistance!"

"Incel Resistance?"

"Incel stands for Involuntary Celibate," explained the driver.

"Watch the road, Todd," chastised Conrad.

"Sorry," Todd demurred.

"I know what an Incel is," Mondel replied. "What are you guys doing?"

"We're fighting against G," explained Conrad. "We're taking the campus back! We hope we can count on your support! We've had a lot of time to think about this. Obviously."

"Look guys, I appreciate what you're trying to do," said Mondel. "But I don't know how much help I can be."

"You have to understand what they're doing up there," Conrad explained. "It's much worse than you think."

"I don't see how that's possible," said Mondel, despondent.

The other student, who still had his mask on, started to show him video clips on his cellphone. In the video, the trans athletes and Antifa members were emptying a dorm and shoving students around.

"They're segregating the dorms," explained the Incel.

"Segregating? By what?" asked Mondel.

"Trans and Queer Fluid got the best dorm assignments, then People of Color, the handi-capable, the women--- All the white straight men were put in the new dorm," he explained.

"All the white men? That's impossible, that would be like---"

"We're 13 to a room, Dr. Mondel," explained Conrad. "We had no choice but to get out. They're monitoring the Internet usage through the school's network and their shaming anyone who watches porn."

In another video, a group of angry girls started screaming up at the window of a male student on his laptop.

"Shame! Shame!" they cried. "You objectify women! Shame!"

The embarrassed student closed his laptop and then the curtain.

"This **cannot** stand, Dr. Mondel," proclaimed Conrad. "This is about freedom, this is about liberty---"

"I haven't jerked it for a week!" added Todd a little shaky. "I'm going crazy!"

"Watch the road, Todd!" insisted Conrad.

"Sorry."

"Anyhow, doc, are you with us?" asked Conrad.

"In spirit, yes," said Mondel, half-committing. "But there's not much I can do!"

"Can't you talk to the town cops?" he asked

"We tried," said Mondel. "But they hate the college. They're only interested in protecting downtown. Look, you guys are outgunned--- They have the numbers."

"We know," said Conrad grimly. "But we're prepared. We've made contact with some of the frat bros, some MRA's and the Campus Libertarians."

"Please don't hurt anybody," Mondel begged. "Things are bad enough as it is. Don't make it worse."

"How much worse can it get, doc? If we don't stand up for ourselves now, then when?" asked Conrad incredulous. "What are we supposed to do? Crawl into that dorm and die? At this point, that's what it seems they want us to do!"

"We have to get the story out somehow," Mondel said holding up the paper. "I tried, my ways are old and useless. You guys know the Internet better than me. I think that's the key."

Mondel paused. What he was about to do seemed completely hypocritical, but he needed to give the boys some tools to help.

"Saul Alinsky, Rules for Radicals," Mondel told them. "That's the book G is using. It should help your cause."

"Rules for Radicals," repeated Conrad. "Thanks doc. I'm sending you a secret email. Contact us only through there if you have anything. We're gonna throw you out now. Try to roll, okay. We wanna make it look like we beat you up."

"Sure. Good luck Incels."

At the next corner, they threw Mondel out onto the street. The van had slowed enough that he merely stumbled as he got out. Mondel balanced himself and started walking back to his car. Along the way, he spotted the town's police station and decided to go in.

The Police Chief was reluctant to see him, but Mondel was insistent and except for the chaos up on the campus, there really wasn't much crime in the area. The Police Chief was a heavy set, old marine about 50 with short graying hair. In the old days, Mondel would've considered him another ignorant jarhead authoritarian. Today, he hoped the man would be his savior and that of the campus.

"Please Chief," begged Mondel. "You have to save the campus. I'm begging you."

"Dr. Mondel, I would like nothing better than to roll up to the Upstate Campus and crack heads until my arms were sore and my hands were bloody," the chief stated. "But that ain't gonna happen."

"Why?"

"While you idiots were dickin' around up on the hill, pretending Communism has a snowball's chance in Hell of workin'--- My officers were patrolling the town. They came up on two black gentlemen spray painting a wall," he told. "Guess what happened next."

"You shot them?" asked Mondel.

"We didn't fuckin' shoot them you idiot!" snapped the chief. "What do you think this is? They attempted to arrest them. They got a little antsy, so my officers tased them."

"I don't see the problem," Mondel commented, not understanding.

The chief pulled out an Ipad and started playing a video of the incident. The two students were painting a mural of Martin Luther King.

"You arrested them for painting a Black History Month mural?" asked Mondel.

"That mural **wasn't** there!" the chief explained. "Those cock-knockers you call students, altered the video somehow!"

"Well, you could just go back to the original wall," thought Mondel. "It's---"

"There's a mural there now," explained the chief. "Those fuckers painted one the next day and now it's been a while. If I go up that hill, your students will release that video to the media and this town's police force is fucked."

The chief threw the Ipad aside in disgust.

"I have cut a deal with G," he explained. "As long as the students stay out of the residential neighborhoods and businesses, I will leave her alone. Until such time that I can destroy that video, my hands are tied."

"Goddammit," said Mondel impressed. "She's a monster."

126

"They," corrected the chief.

Chapter 27

Mondel got back to his place and set the headlight on the kitchen table. He immediately called Jared.

"Hey, buddy!" he greeted.

"Jared, you fucking asshole!" shouted Mondel. "How can you fucking do this to me?! You used to be my best friend!"

"Whoa-whoa, calm down," said Jared, who skipped out of the end of an editorial meeting to talk. "Don't worry, we're going to get your side of the story."

"My side?! My side?! You told me Freidman was going to talk to **me**! He spent two paragraphs calling me the reincarnation of Hitler and he never talked to me once!" Mondel screamed. "You actually printed libel! I'm going to sue you and the paper!"

"First off, he didn't libel you," assured Jared. "That's an opinion piece."

"You put it on the front page!" shouted Mondel. "Since when do you put an Op-ed on the front page?!"

"Journalism has changed," Jared offered.

"Op-ed's aren't journalism! Any moron with a word processor and a working brain cell can write one! Freidman didn't investigate anything!" snapped Mondel.

"Yeah, the guy's a hardcore Marxist," admitted Jared. "He just **loved** your students."

"You fucked me, Jared! You fucked me!" screamed Mondel, more furious than he had ever been. "I'll never be able to work anywhere else again!"

"I thought you have tenure."

"I do have tenure!"

"Look, buddy, you have to understand, Freidman gets hits," Jared said, explaining the new dynamic. "The hits on his article were through the roof! It's captured national attention, we can't stop that."

"It captured national attention because you're telling a lie!" pointed out Mondel. "The students are destroying the campus!"

"That's not what I heard," said Jared simply.

"Because you have no idea what's happening!"

"Look, there's going to be more reporters coming and I'm sure one of them is going to talk to you," Jared said. "You just need to make sure you have a really good hook for them. If your hook is better, then problem solved! We just need to get a 24-hour news cycle out of it."

"You're unbelievable," Mondel said, full of rage. "You lie to everyone and then you ask me to create a better lie so you can get ratings and cover it?!"

"It's the way things work now, buddy," he explained. "Facts are facts, but hits are king. Gotta go. Text me sometime."

Mondel was too wound up to replace his headlight. He wanted to get back at Jared and prove him wrong. Truth had to exist. The truth was real and he had always believed it was more powerful than any propagandist narrative. He went on the Internet.

Every major news outlet was repeating the narrative. A brave, innocent member of the LGBTQ community was viciously attacked by her college, only to rise above it and turn the tables. The story had every juicy bit the readers could stand: a marginalized protagonist, a powerful institution and an against-all-odds plot right out of a movie.

And who were the readers of the Press of New York? College educated elites who had been taught for generations to protest. That institutions were staid, corrupt edifices to be torn down and remade in the image of the young. This Collective, with all the trappings of a Communist "Utopia" had to work. "True Communism had never been tried!" was the rallying cry of the campus Commie. It took someone as bright, smart and wonderful as G.

The only problem was, Mondel knew she wasn't wonderful. She was no more immune to the corruption of power than anyone else. Her excesses were already on display, it was the media that refused to see them. That's the narrative he needed to dispel. That she was different from anyone else.

But to do so, he would get no help from the papers, television or Cable TV news. These dead mediums were too busy feeding at the Internet trough in a vain attempt to postpone their inevitable demise into rarely visited websites full of clickbait ads and links to Amazon.

Mondel searched for independent voices. Were there any left on YouTube since the great VoxAdpocalypse? Here and there, pundits did takes on the Upstate College event. They were mostly conservatives with audiences too small for Google to be worried about. They seemed sympathetic, if a little nutty sometimes, but none of them had any evidence.

The truly bizarre video was one from a razor company called Stay Sharp. They were struggling to gain a share in the very crowded woke razor market, so they announced they would ship free razors to help G's cause. They even produced a slick ad parodying World War 2 propaganda movies with a voice over like this:

News that keeps you sharp!

Dateline! Upstate College where a group of inclusive students who are gay and trans struggle to be heard! (The ad featured video of the students from Freidman's online piece with the old black and white film effect layered on top.) But don't worry kids! Stay Sharp Razors is supporting your fight against fascism with our sharpest of razors! Shipped to you absolutely free! (There was footage of a truck delivering the razors to the dining hall.) Good luck, G! And keep fighting! Because we all want to create an inclusive world! And for the ones that don't--- (The video ended with a clip of Mondel saying, "That's Fascism!") Stay Sharp Razors! Look good, feel good and stay woke!

Mondel frowned and then sighed. He was really getting sick of seeing that clip of himself.

Then the doctor stumbled upon some students who had taken cellphone video and uploaded it. They attended Upstate and had clips from the previous weeks. Some of them had to have captured the events. At the very least, they might have something that could prove useful to help take down G.

YouTube's search kept showing him major network coverage of the campus. It was full of glowing praise for G and her cohorts. He realized he had to search through pages of results to get to actual video that criticized anything. Finally, he found it! It was clear video of the Milkshake incident! One of the students had captured G eyeing up Greizer and then hurling the milkshake at him. She even gave a thumbs up to the camera and mouthed the words "Fuck that guy!"

He yawned and saved the link. Having spent hours on YouTube to find it, all that was left to be done was to figure out how best to use it. He emailed the link to the Incels. At this point, who cares? This situation was so far out of control now, Mondel couldn't possibly see it getting any worse.

Chapter 28

Without the intervention of the local authorities, the assistant deans were beside themselves. Over a dozen faculty members started burning through vacation time or taking leaves of absence to avoid coming to work. The students had welcomed certain woke professors like Karen and Gwendolyn, who traveled back and forth from campus with ease. Fawkes stayed and never left.

The deans called an emergency faculty meeting in the only space still owned by the college, but off campus. The Troubadour Building. Mondel picked up the Professor. P stopped and noted the condition of his car. He refrained from asking what happened.

"Where is this building?" asked Mondel as he got in the car.

"You don't know? Hmph, guess it was before your time," said Papadopoulos. "The college used to have an all men's a cappella singing club. Used to bring in the donors. They shut it down in the 70's for being sexist."

"Are we talking about going back to campus and trying to teach?" asked Mondel.

"I guess that's an option, but fuck if I'm going to do it," said P. "Maybe if I was your age, but I don't standing a fighting chance if those assholes corner me. And I'm on their list."

"What list?"

"Oh, you didn't hear?" laughed P bitterly. "G's minions hacked the college's website so she can spout her nonsense 24/7. Made a list of problematic teachers that have to answer for microaggressions or some such."

"Oh, no," Mondel said horrified.

"Don't worry, you didn't make the cut for some reason."

"I didn't?' said Mondel curiously.

"No," said P suspiciously.

The Troubadour Building was a large rehearsal space and performance hall that was hardly ever used by the college anymore. The Music Department had a bigger facility up on the hill, despite the old wood feel of the recital hall. The remaining faculty members were a raucous mob standing in the audience, while the four deans attempted to address their concerns.

"All right everyone, all right!" shouted Maxine Washington, the most willful of the four. "We're here to discuss ways to move forward! Screaming your complaints at us is not going to be constructive! Now we have gone over the town cops to the county and the state officials and so far, they are unwilling to get involved."

"They've taken over the Science Department," explained Wes. "They say if we don't teach that the world is going to end in ten years because of climate change, they'll burn down the building. Talk about a carbon tax. Amirite?"

"You've got to rein in these lunatics!" insisted one agitated professor. "I had a student turn in a **used tampon** as a Midterm paper!"

"They looted the bookstore! How are we supposed to get royalties now? We're going to have to release a new edition!" cried another.

"Those smug little shits hacked my Facebook profile and replaced all my pictures with Hitler!" another said, outraged. "Arrest them!"

The room was in agreement. It had gone too far. But Mondel already knew the local cops wouldn't help. Karen, Gwendolyn and another professor named Willow, moved to the front to address the mob.

"Everyone, we should seek to **learn** from this experience," offered Karen.

A roar went up in the room. They thought she was crazy.

"We've been working with these students, along with Professor Fawkes and they have a lot to teach us!" she insisted.

"I think you have it backwards, Karen," noted Maxine.

Mondel noticed that one of the assistant deans had a lap top and a projector. He was going to do a six point presentation on why they should all wait out the school year. Mondel walked up on stage.

"Everyone! Everyone!" he shouted over the crowd. "We have to fight the narrative! G has controlled the message from the very beginning! Manipulated the perception of people. We need to take that back! And I have just the thing. May I?"

Mondel used the laptop to call up the YouTube link.

"This is the proof we can use to fight G and expose her for the fraud she is," Mondel announced proudly.

132

Clicking the link, the page came up "This video is no longer available because the YouTube account associated with this video has been terminated."

"What? No!" cried Mondel, trying to find another copy of the video.

But it had been scrubbed from the platform and straight down the Memory Hole. If could take weeks to find a copy of the clip, if it still existed. Professor P looked embarrassed for him and the room erupted in angry yells again.

"We should join they!" insisted Karen, over the objections. "They is creating something wonderful!"

"Karen, you will not encourage these students any further!" insisted Maxine.

The indignant three professors looked angry. They didn't like to be told no on anything. Karen nodded to the other two and they started walking out.

"Where are you going Karen? Karen? Gwen?" the assistant dean called after them over the mob.

"Wait! Wait! Wait!" shouted Mondel as the three women left. "We still have one ace in the hole!"

"What?" asked Wes.

"The truth," argued Mondel.

The room scoffed.

"We're all teachers, but--- We've always held back. We've always protected these kids from the harsh realities of life. We need to go back up on the hill and tell those students the harshest, most real realities of this world. And teach them like we never taught them before!" proclaimed Mondel pointing up the hill.

"Yeah!" shouted Professor P. "Truth! Truth! Truth!"

The faculty started chanting "Truth!" over and over. And for the first time, Mondel saw of sliver of light in the darkness. The assistant deans shrugged. Guess this was better than making a decision.

Karen, Gwendolyn and Willow headed back to campus in Karen's Kia. They told themselves they were joining G's Collective, but this was a lie. They were already full fledged members who had actively participated in the discussions of things like how to secretly get salt peter into the water supply of the male dorms. They found G in the dining hall explaining her latest innovation.

"Karen, Gwen, Willow," she greeted. "You're just in time. We're going to institute a system to prevent misgendering. These name tags will be printed on official PBC printers and required for all students to wear."

"Innovative!" gushed Karen immediately.

133

She noted the sample yellow name tags on the table. They including cis-hetero males and females, gay, lesbian, intersex and then divisions based on race and religion. There were hundreds of labels, including some of the more recently discovered genders. The last few tags looked a little faded.

"We're running low on toner," G explained. "But we should be able to acquire some from the faculty offices, right?"

Karen smiled. Of course she'd raid the office supplies for them. This was more important than whatever faculty nonsense a patriarchal institution like Upstate would use them for.

"But wait, where are the trans tags?" she asked, scanning the table.

"Karen," said G, watching her reaction carefully. "Trans women are women."

"Now just a second!" objected Gwendolyn.

"Gwen," Karen calmed her. "G, we talked about this. My sisters here fought for women's rights and---"

"Are you saying that I'm not a woman?" Chloe demanded, stepping forward.

"You're pre-op, you have a penis," Karen pointed out.

"A woman's penis!" pointed out Penny. "We have no room in the Collective for TERFs, Karen!"

"That kind of hate isn't welcomed here," said G.

Karen's mouth dropped open. She had supported G since the beginning. She was the one that gave her the heads up about the speaker coming to campus. Now she felt the whole room turn against her and her fellow lesbian sisters.

"We laid the groundwork for you!" shouted Willow. "Without us, none of this would be possible!"

"And we thank you for that, but your history is over," said G dismissive. "It's time to make new history. **Our** history."

"You won't last a day without our support!" Karen threatened. "C'mon girls."

Karen looked over to Charlene, the grad student. She'd been watching from a distance as the argument broke out.

"Charlene, you're coming, right?" asked Karen.

"Um, you guys," Charlene laughed nervously. "It doesn't have to come to this."

Karen turned and walked away with Gwen and Willow.

"That's it!" shouted Chloe. "Get lost, Third Wave!"

"Oh, Karen," said G, calling them back and holding up a nametag that said 'lesbian'. "Don't forget your sticker."

Chapter 29

The next morning, the professors returned to Upstate with their plan. Professor P had called ahead of time and spoke with Penny.

"The faculty is coming back to campus to teach," the professor informed her. "We don't expect any violence. Do you?"

Penny put her phone to her chest and informed G. The professors were coming to her turf now. They had the home field advantage. What could they do? She would grind them down just as she had done with Fawkes and the others. She nodded in approval and pointed to the name tags.

"As long as your professors adhere to the new dress code," she informed him. "You'll be given gender tags at the gate."

Mondel arrived the next morning and one of the Antifa members stopped him.

"Gender?" he asked curtly.

"Uh, male," he replied.

"Orientation?"

"Straight."

"Are you Jewish?" he asked, unsure.

"Why don't you just put our names?" he asked.

"Are you a Jew or not?" he demanded.

"I'm not wearing a tag that says I'm a Jew!" he snapped. "What next? A Yellow Star that says Juden on it?"

"I don't get the reference," he said confused.

"Of course you don't, Ben!" Mondel snapped, grabbing the name tag out of his hands. "You failed the History of World War 2!"

With the line of cars honking and so many tags to check, Ben was exhausted and let the doctor go. Mondel got to K lot, but found the spaces covered in snow. Across the way, one of the new student maintenance people had tried to drive the snow plow down an outside staircase. It dug the plow into the asphalt at the bottom and was now stuck there with its back wheels unable to get traction. The students had just left it there. The other plow had rolled into the lake when the Antifa driver failed to put the parking brake on. Now nothing was getting cleared. The faculty parked along the main access road where the snow wasn't too deep. Mondel got out and headed for his class.

The campus was in a shambles. A broken window at one of the doors had been replaced by a taped up garbage bag. The student union's broken windows had been covered by mismatched lumber the students had scrounged from a maintenance shed. It wasn't nailed up, it was just leaning against the holes propped up by several cases of Stay Sharp razors. The lights in the classrooms were flickering on and off. Before the students had wrecked the snowplows, they had smashed into one of the transformers with the vehicle and never told anyone about it. The heat went off in the library and some of the pipes had frozen, making the bathrooms useless. It didn't stop the students from using the facilities when they were there, however.

Mondel got into the hall and found the snack vending machines were completely empty. One had been knocked over and smashed open. A few pennies were lying on the rug near by. Walking through the lights of the flickering hall, he reached the door to his classroom, which had the words "Fuck Mondel!" spray painted on them. Mondel sighed and went in. He found a group of six out of twenty of his students from the Poly-Sci 101 Class. Five of the boys and one heavily tattooed girl.

"See? I told you he'd come," said Tyler as he entered.

"Thank God!" cried Kyle. "Thank God!"

"Dr. Mondel, Kyle wanted to talk to you during office hours, but I figured you could just do it here," said Tyler.

"Well, if it's private…"

"It's doesn't matter!" cried Kyle. "I'm going crazy! Everybody knows! Everybody knows!"

"Knows what?" asked Mondel.

"His girlfriend has forced him into being a cuckold," explained Tyler, as Kyle wept.

"I did everything she said!" cried Kyle. "And now Heather is doing it with some other guy! She says I have to accept it! That it's what a modern relationship is like! Oh, God!"

"Kyle, you have to get a hold yourself," said Mondel. "There are plenty of other fish in the sea."

"Are there?!" he said bitterly. "Heather and I have been dating since the tenth grade! I was gonna ask her to marry me at graduation!"

"Just calm down," Mondel said, offering him a bottle of water he brought from home. "Listen to me, as a divorced guy, marriage is not the answer."

"I figured she would calm down after we were married," said Kyle. "Once we had a kid, she'd give all this feminism stuff up."

"That's not the way it works," Mondel explained. "Women are not attracted to guys that do everything they say. Rosanna, back me up here."

Rosanna, who was leaning on her hands, suddenly piped up curious. Were they actually having this conversation?

"Uh, yeah, I guess," she said.

"Tell the truth, are you going to be attracted to soy-boy Kyle here or some rough biker guy you just met at a bar who looks like he either just got out or is going to prison."

Rosanna blushed.

"Biker. Ding-ding-ding," she laughed.

"Evolution, Kyle!" shouted Mondel. "We are all just creatures. Men evolved to hunt and provide. We seek out the young, fertile girls. Even guys my age, you think we don't look at Victoria's Secret catalogue and wanna fuck those girls?"

The class was riveted. Mondel had never felt so free standing in front of a group of students.

"Women are attracted to strength and confidence!" Mondel told Kyle. "Stop being a pussy! It doesn't mean you have to be an asshole and hit her, but it means you have to act like a man! Stop crying!"

Kyle tried pulling himself together. He desperately attempted to hold back the tears.

"From now on in this class and in all classes, we deal with nothing but truth!" proclaimed Mondel. "Nothing is off limits! Nothing can't be discussed! Ask me anything! I will give you my honest answer, no matter how ugly, dark and disgusting it may be!"

Throughout the campus, the professors that had shown up for work at Upstate were doing the same thing. They had turned on the spigot of unbridled honesty and told the students the dark secrets of adulthood.

"If you wanna fuck yourself," explained an economic teacher. "Buy a house with an adjustable mortgage. You think you're paying for school loans now? Wait until you're staring down the barrel of a thirty year mortgage! I'll be 72 when my house is paid. I don't even plan on **living** that long!"

"Don't **ever** have kids," the sociology professor ranted. "My vagina looks like a ham sandwich flapping in the breeze thanks to the big headed little shit I gave birth to! Do I love my son? I **have** to love my son! I have to keep telling myself that every night so I can justify my life and not drive off a goddamned cliff every day!"

"Most of you are not special," lectured Professor P. "You will not accomplish great things and, in fact, most of you are pieces of shit. The best you can do is to try to be less pieces of shit. Understand? If most of you just tried to do the bare minimum of not fucking up everything for the rest of us, then the smart people could get things accomplished. Get out of the way! Stop being selfish, stupid, self-absorbed assholes and think about anyone else for once in your miserable lives!"

"None of you has enough talent to make a career in music," explained the music teacher to his class. "Not **one** of you. If you did, you wouldn't be here. You wanna know who could get a record deal in this room? This girl! Stand up please."

One of the flute players was absolutely stunning. She was a shy blonde with big eyes and enormous breasts.

"This girl right here could have a record deal because she could have **anything she wants**!" explained the teacher in frustration. "Look at her! I would give everything I have to be with her! Looks do matter!"

"I got into teaching," explained Wes to his class. "Because I am a lazy piece of shit. I don't like working, I don't care about my students and this is the easiest job I've ever had. Teaching is a scam designed to sell books. If I knew what I know about this job back when I was your age, I seriously would've just sold drugs."

"The government is out to fuck you!" proclaimed Mondel. "They've always fucked over their constituencies! There isn't a cunt hair's difference between the Republican and Democratic parties! You know what they agree on? Each year Congress gives themselves a raise on us! They enrich their crony friends and families by giving them contracts and information! Hell, it was legal to do insider trading in Congress up until a few years ago! Anyone who would willingly run for office is the exact kind of sociopath that shouldn't be anywhere near the levers of power!"

"Cops are assholes," proclaimed the law professor. "But we lawyers are just parasites on productive society. I wish cancer on any of my students that became divorce attorneys. Those people would fuck their own mothers."

"Television and movies are dead!" proclaimed the communications teacher. "And the studio corporations control everything! There hasn't been a real newscast since the 70's!"

"Most people don't have an original thought in their head!" proclaimed the writing professor.

"The world is so completely fucked up!" Professor P preached.

"Life is not fair," said Diana. "Everything is stacked against you!"

"You're all gonna die," said Wes simply. "Some of you within a few years, statistically."

"Love is a lie and marriage is a trap," proclaimed the economics teacher.

"Trust no one!" shouted the law professor.

"Don't **ever** have kids!" begged sociology teacher. "Seriously, I wish I had sterilized myself."

"No one ever gets ahead. Being an adult is the constant stress of worrying about will I be destitute and homeless tomorrow because no one is going to care if that happens! No one!" proclaimed Mondel, flopping down in his seat.

There was a long pause as the students in his class started to process the hard truths Mondel had ranted about.

"That was--- Wow," laughed Tyler. "I am a little numb."

"I knew we were fucked," said Rosanna, smiling that her theories on life had been validated. "I knew it! I'm just so glad someone finally **said** it."

"You got my mind off my immediate troubles," said Kyle, who was no longer crying but was mildly horrified. "Now I'm worried about so much more."

"When's the campus going to be fixed, Dr. Mondel?" asked Tyler. "Why haven't the cops come?"

"Bottom line Tyler," explained Mondel. "Everyone in the outside world has their head so far up their ass smelling their own farts, they want to believe what G is doing is exciting and good. My advice, get out of this college as soon as possible."

"I'm down with that," said Rosanna agreeing. "The heat's off in my dorm and the cafeteria is running out of food."

"Hey," said Tyler. "Help me dig my car out of the snow and we'll go."

"Where?" she asked intrigued.

"Fuck if I know," he smiled back.

"My parents told me to stay here," confessed Kyle.

"Fuck your parents," Mondel dismissed. "Go home."

Chapter 30

Later, inside the faculty offices, the professor were sharing Mondel's bottle of whiskey. They were laughing and talking about the reaction of their students to the terrible news about future adulthood.

"You've should've seen the looks on their faces!" laughed Professor P. "When I told them what I actually paid in taxes last year vs. how much I make. They went pale as shit!"

"One girl in my class wants to be a lawyer and raise a baby at the same time," laughed Diana. "I told her, on what planet do you think you're going to be able to work ten hours a day and raise a kid? You ever try to breastfeed at work? And say goodbye to your social life! She didn't know what to say!"

Chloe and a few Antifa members suddenly burst into the room. They were led by Olivia, who looked frazzled and overwhelmed.

"You have to get out of here," she told the professors.

Beyond the doorway, Mel Franklin lurked. He avoided Professor P's gaze and walked away.

"Why? That asshole Franklin tell you to do that?" said P defiantly.

"We're turning off the electricity, so that there's more power to the rest of the school," she explained.

"That doesn't make any sense," said Diana. "That's not how a power grid---"

"Don't question it!" she snapped. "We're in charge, not you! Now are you leaving or do we have to throw you out?"

There was an odd tension in the room. Mondel was so high on what he had accomplished today, he didn't see it. Professor P did and gestured for him not to respond.

"Okay, we'll go," said the professor.

The faculty gathered their belongings as the impatient students watched. The Antifa members were holding batons and slapping them in their hands menacingly. Finally, the group walked out and one of the black clad students slammed the door and locked it after them.

"What the Hell was that all about?" asked Mondel, still oblivious.

"She knows," explained Professor P. "We told the students hard truths and it got back to G. In an empire of lies, we committed the only crime. It was a good attempt, Lawrence, but I don't think it can reverse what's happened here."

Professor P started walking to his vehicle.

"I have a back up plan," he explained. "Let's all meet at the bar downtown. I'll text you ahead of time. And everyone, please, watch your backs getting to your car."

The mood had suddenly turned ugly. Mondel escorted Diana back to her car and then headed for his. He wished he hadn't parked so far away. Now he had to traverse the campus.

As he headed for the road near K lot, he noticed a student trying to drive a bulldozer next to one of the dorms. While other students watched, he pushed it into the side of the building, damaging the wall. Mondel went running over.

"What the Hell are you guys doing?" demanded Mondel. "You're going to collapse the building!"

"Please, Dr. Mondel. This is the reeducation camp," said Fawkes, who Mondel realized was one of the group. "You can't interrupt the process."

"What process?!" he demanded.

"Look, I'm not supposed to talk to any more white heteros if I can help it but, we're building a new entrance for people of color. Then we're building one for women, the intersex, the queer fluid--- About thirteen ought to do it."

"Plus the handicapable ramp!" added a student.

"Yes! Very good, Jeremy!" Fawkes complimented.

"Fawkes, you've lost it!" snapped Mondel. "You're going to get someone killed!"

"We're just dedicated to the Cause," Fawkes assured him cheerfully. "Once we're finished with this, we have to expand all the women's bathrooms! Did you know, the line to the women's bathroom is always longer than the men's room? That's Patriarchy!"

For a second, Mondel wished he had been recording that, if only to replace the viral video of himself.

"You guys are gonna collapse the building! You're not even wearing hard hats!" Mondel objected.

"Yeah, on that you got us!" Fawkes said. "One of the other cucks got hit by a brick, but the PBC ambulance took him, so it's okay."

141

"Ambulance? The school doesn't have an ambulance," said Mondel.

At that moment, the two Antifa members that drove Fawkes' Prius, were dropping the injured student at the hospital's emergency entrance. They kicked him out of the car and drove off.

"Good luck, cuck!" laughed the driver.

The injured student staggered a few steps, then collapsed in the doorway. A nurse poked her head out and then ran outside to help.

"Fawkes, listen to me!" Mondel said, trying to reach him. "This is barbaric! You have to help these students and get them out of here!"

It was then, Mondel noticed Fawkes looked emaciated and pale.

"Wait, are they not feeding you?" he asked.

"We're sacrificing for the good of the collective!" he assured pleasantly. "It's all for a good cause!"

The bulldozer hit the side of the building and a huge chunk tumbled down. Inside, a surprised Santos was masturbating to something on his laptop. He struggled to get his pants up, carry the computer and run away.

"I'm struggling!" he said. "I'm a struggling feminist!"

"Goddess speed!" said Fawkes cheerfully, wishing him well. "Ah, good feminist."

Mondel felt compelled to run away from the insanity. He took the snowy, unplowed road off campus. He passed a group of students burning books in an oil drum, trying to keep themselves warm. At the lower quads, where some of the upper classman lived, it was chaos. When the wifi and cable TV finally stopped, lawlessness prevailed. Some were getting high, while others were robbing each other for food, drugs and valuables. There were, however, an over abundance of razors since cases of the Stay Sharp Razors had been left in front of every dorm.

Mondel went back to his place and watched the news reports. The major network most closely associated with left politics held an interview with G and hailed her as a visionary. She basked in the adulation, promising that all the students at Upstate College were now safe, well-educated and happy. Anyone that said otherwise was clearly a bigot, racist, homophobe troll whose opinion needn't be entertained in the slightest.

"Any word on Dr. Lawrence Mondel, the man who started it all?" asked the host.

"I imagine Dr. Mondel lives in a very lonely world of his own creation," G said smugly. "Imagine how it is to be so hate-filled and narrow minded? I truly pity him."

The network posted yet another still from the video to make it look like he was doing the Hitler salute.

142

"Truly sad," said the host.

Mondel's phone rang. It was a number he didn't recognize, but with all the confusion--- He thought it might be the Incel Resistance reaching out to him or even one of the students. He answered.

"Hello?" he said warily.

"Lawrence?" said Celia.

"Celia?" said Mondel surprised. "Are you okay? You're not on campus are you?"

"Yeah, I'm getting ready for this play," she said routinely. "Look, I feel terrible about the way I just brushed you off, but I wanted to invite you to the opening."

"Celia, you have to get off campus," warned Mondel. "It's coming unglued."

"I know, that's what some trolls on the Internet say, but we've got power and heat in the theater, so---"

"Celia, I'm not kidding," warned Mondel. "You should get out."

"Look, I can't leave the kids, they worked too hard," she said sympathizing. "But if you're around, stop by the play. Starts at seven. Okay? Bye."

"Celia--- Hello?"

It was like Celia was living in a different world. And, to some extent, she was. Penny, under G's orders, had made sure the theater was getting all the electricity, water and food that was available. The play, now that it was rewritten, had to go on.

Mondel got a text from P: "Come to the bar. Now."

143

Chapter 31

Mondel got to parking garage, but Homeless Vic had already gone home for the night. He looked down the street, the bars and restaurants that catered to the students had been trashed. Fights were breaking out between the Antifa members and the bouncers. No one was paying their bills anymore. The students had decided that the evils of Capitalism had to be fought by dining and dashing. The cops, who were only now interested in protecting the businesses that didn't cater to the students, felt the bar owners had betrayed the town. They let their 911 calls go unanswered.

Fortunately, Upstate Downstairs was not one of those places. The bar had a large bouncer who nodded in approval and opened the door when the doctor approached. Mondel rushed in and found Diana and the Professor sitting in a booth.

"It's spreading to the town," Mondel noted.

"We know," said Diana. "That's why the Professor's plan is the best."

"Okay, what's the plan?" asked Mondel.

"We leave and we sue the school," Professor P said excitedly. "I'm talking class action lawsuit, the entire faculty. Whatever millions that fuck up Albert has squirreled away for construction? Right in our pockets! It'll take a few years, but we'll be set for life! After the truth comes out about this fiasco! Haha!"

Mondel sat back in the booth. Deflated.

"What? What the Hell is wrong?" asked P.

"I can't."

"You can't? What do you mean you can't?!" snapped P.

"It's over, Lawrence," Diana said. "Wes already left with his family."

"But I have tenure," said Mondel, starting to cry.

"We all do! So what?" said P. "Jesus Christ, Lawrence! We have to get out of here before this Commie Clusterfuck blows up in our faces!"

"It's my school," he cried. "I grew up here, met my wife here, started a career here. This is my life!"

"Those days are gone," Diana said gently.

"Lawrence, wake up!" said the Professor, trying to reach him. "These sensitive kids with their safe spaces and precious egos--- The writing's been on the wall since you were a student!"

"What?" said Mondel, not making the connection.

"Oh, you don't remember the 90's when rap music was going to destroy the country and the precious PMRC **saved** everyone with warning labels on record albums? Or how about the warnings on TV shows? Thank God we protected the kids from seeing a titty or hearing shit-fuck on the news!" ranted P. "More than 80% of the people of the world live on less than $10 a day, Lawrence! These kids spend more than that on Spotify or Starbucks! You think any of them could change a tire or balance a checking account? They have a fucking nervous breakdown if you use the wrong pronoun on Twitter!"

"But they're just kids---"

"A hundred years ago, they'd already have fucking families and jobs and polio, if they hadn't died in a war! Now they can't figure out how to change a goddamned light bulb without watching a tutorial on YouTube!" shouted P, now ranting at top volume. "I swear to Christ, I wish people were still religious and this is **me** saying it! Those Christian fuckers tried to fuck me and all my kind--- Throw us in jail or convert us, but **fuck**! At least they had some kind of belief system that didn't just assume all their bills would somehow magically be paid! At least they weren't tearing down the fabric of fucking society! At least there was something left to change!"

"We can make corrections in the system!" insisted Mondel.

"**There is no fucking system now!** Between Albert's greed and the ego of the Regents and the unmitigated arrogance of the students--- We're the only ones pretending a fucking college still exists!" he shouted. "Do you think for one second that these cocksucking helicopter parents will admit one iota of fault?! No! They'll blame us! They always blame the teachers! That's how the system got so fucked, trying to pass off their kid's dysfunction as a fucking reason to keep coddling them! Well, fuck them, Lawrence! Fuck their kids! Let them deal with their stoner idiot children in their old age while they squander the family fortune! They made their bed, let them fucking lie in it! It's time all the generations got what's coming to them! Maybe the coming chaos will finally cull the fucking herd again!"

Mondel sat in silence as the Professor panted from his long diatribe.

"I'm sorry. I wish you well," said the doctor, getting up.

"Lawrence!" the Professor called after him. "Don't be a fool! You can't go back there! Lawrence!"

But Mondel wasn't listening, he walked out of the bar in a daze. He went into an alley, leaned against the wall and started crying.

"Hey! Dr. Mondel? That you?" said a voice.

Mondel turned. It was Homeless Vic.

"Hey, doc!" he greeted, walking out of the darkness.

"I'm sorry, Vic. I'm just---"

"Hey, don't worry about it!" he laughed. "Come with me! Time to pay it forward!"

With nowhere else to go, Mondel followed Vic down the alley. He eventually came to a warehouse entrance on the other block. Vic opened a door and beckoned him inside. If the homeless vet was going to stab and rob him, this would be a perfect time--- A perfect way to end the shittiest night of his life. He followed.

Inside, there was a group of local drug dealers and low level criminals. They were seated around a space heater on boxes of Stay Sharp Razors. There were hundreds of the boxes stacked in the warehouse. The group was drinking bottles of Ms. Stout, eating stolen food from the Vegan V and smoking pot. A particularly mean guy in a knit cap named Jules, picked up a Glock and aimed it at Mondel threateningly.

"Who the fuck is this?!" demanded Jules.

"Calm your shit down, Jules!" Vic ordered. "This here's my niggah, Mondel!"

"Is he cool?" asked Jules suspiciously.

"Yeah-yeah," Mondel said nervously.

"You know how many dollars this motherfucker gave me over the years?!" said Vic. "I'd be dead without him!"

"Thanks, Vic," thanked Mondel.

"No problem, doc. Here you go," he said handing him a bottle of whiskey.

Mondel took a sip to be sociable, expecting it to burn. It was actually some of the smoothest whiskey he had ever tasted.

"Damn," he said impressed.

"Yeah, that shit's $500 a bottle," laughed Vic. "We rollin' in it, thanks to you."

"Thanks to me?" said Mondel, not understanding.

"Yeah, since all the bullshit that happened at the college, the cops don't come down here no more," explained Jules.

"We do whatever the fuck we want now," explained a thuggish bald guy with tattoos. "And the college pussy is everywhere!"

The group laughed.

"I hear that!" agreed Vic. "My girl Heather is sweeeeeeet!"

"You guys have college girlfriends?" asked Mondel, mildly confused.

"Nah, it's the craziest thing," said Vic.

"Them white bitches come down off the hill looking for real men to give it to them," explained Jules. "They all got boyfriends that let them fuck? **That's** fucked up!"

"And they let us do everything," the bald tattooed guy remembered. "That chick, Penny, is a **freak**!"

"I know! I know!" agreed Jules. "We all know!"

"What kind of man let his woman do that?" laughed Vic. "What do you teach them college boys, Mondel?"

"I don't know anymore," the doctor said lost. "If you don't mind me asking, where did you get all the money?"

"Mostly reselling these razors," said Jules. "The trucks just keep dropping them off at the school and we boost them. Those students are afraid of us. Some of them we rob. They're just college students, they piss their pants when they see this."

Jules waved around the gun. Mondel tensed up.

"It's not even loaded!" he laughed.

"And I've been sellin' mad amounts of chronic and other shit up on the hill," confessed bald and tattooed. "My sales have **tripled** since the shit went down. You need anything doc, you just let us know. Any dawg of Vic's is our dawg."

"Hell, we're making so much money, maybe we'll go to college!" joked Vic.

The group laughed. Mondel smiled half-heartedly.

After lingering with them for another twenty minutes, Vic handed him a free case of Stay Sharp Razors. Mondel sadly carried them back to his car. As he walked down the sidewalk, he flashbacked to his college days:

He remembered getting drunk with Professor P one night at the Downstairs. He remembered taking Brianna on dates downtown. He went to the movies with Jared and his other friends and then rushed back to class. The ghost of his college experience haunted him. He thought those experiences would be universal to everyone, but now it seemed it was from a time long past. An era of humanity and education had withered away under the relentless assault of the politics of eliminating risk.

Mondel thought that he too had been coddled by his parents in his own way. Each generation before had had it tougher and wanted to make it easier on the next. But somewhere, society had reached a tipping point turning their brood into unctuous spoiled babies. The kind that would break their own toys while demanding newer ones.

As much as it would benefit him to leave, Mondel would stay. He'd stay until G ground down the last stone on the hill. It was his college and she was the interloper. He'd rather die than give her the satisfaction of driving him away.

Chapter 32

Mondel returned to his apartment, drained of energy and sleepy from good whiskey. He flopped down on the couch and promptly fell asleep with the box of razors under his arm.

"Doc?" whispered a voice. "Doc, don't freak out."

Suddenly aware that someone was inside his apartment, Mondel abruptly stood. It was the Incel Resistance and a student named Derrick.

"Conrad?" he said dazed. "What are you guys doing in here?"

"We wanted to sneak in, but we don't know how to pick locks," admitted Conrad.

"We owe you a back door window," explained Todd.

"This is Derrick from the Campus Libertarians," Conrad introduced.

"The Sons of Liberty, dude," reminded Derrick.

"Oh, very nice," said Mondel, getting it.

"See? He gets it," Derrick said. "Doc, here's a ticket to the play tonight. We got you a seat right next to the audio visual guy. At exactly 7:13, we're going to create a distraction. We need you to rush over to audio visual guy's laptop and plug in this flash drive."

"What? Why?"

"It's going to expose G for who she really is," smiled Conrad.

"You guys got it? Oh, thank God!" said Mondel smiling.

He hugged the Incel Resistance members.

"You guys! I had lost all hope! Thank you!" said Mondel.

"Hey, 4chan gave us all the ammo we need," said Conrad.

"So you'll do it?" confirmed Derrick.

"Of course! Just put it in?"

"Yeah, it'll start playing a presentation," explained Derrick. "Just make sure no one smashes the laptop before it's done."

"I'll die before that happens," promised Mondel.

"Is this guy not the best teacher on campus?" asked Conrad.

"You're right," agreed Derrick. "When all this is over, I'm switching advisers to you, doc!"

That night, Mondel drove up the hill. The Antifa members were no longer guarding the entrance. Two were standing by the roadside, trying to keep warm by a fire. They noticed the cars, but did nothing.

As Mondel drove in, he saw that most of the buildings on campus looked dark. One of them appeared to be scarred with a fire that had burned out and another had a river of water flowing out the front door, which froze in an ice ramp on the sidewalk. He could still see a few lights in the dorms up on the hill, but they appeared to be flashlights or other small lamps, not the actual lights from the buildings. Only the dining hall, one of the dorms and the theater seemed to have power at this point. One of the Safety and Security cruisers had crashed into a fire hydrant. The water coming out of the ground had frozen it in place and the doors were left open.

Mondel couldn't find a place to park. Some of the students directed him and a few other drivers to what looked like an open field that seemed pretty icy, but flat. Mondel was the last person in the new lot as the other theater goers went ahead inside. After walking away from his car several feet, he heard crunching underneath and looked down. It was then, he realized he was standing on the edge of the lake. Ice started cracking and he turned around. His car, along with the other dozen or so vehicles suddenly broke through the surface and sank into the freezing water below. Mondel sighed and headed inside the theater.

Mx. Butterfly had tight security. The biggest Antifa members and trans athletes searched everyone on the way in. Fortunately, they didn't know the first thing about frisking people. They were just interested to make sure that everyone had the right name tag on. Mondel forgot his, so one of the Antifa guys wrote "Fascism Guy" on a sticker, pressed it on his jacket and laughed. Mondel walked to his seat, taking off the name tag once he had moved sufficiently far away.

Sitting down, Mondel immediately took notice of the audio visual guy. He was right where the Incel Resistance said. Mondel checked his watch.

"Hey, Lawrence!" greeted Celia, suddenly walking over. "Thanks for making the trek! I didn't think you would come."

"Oh, well, I love live theater," said Mondel.

150

"Me too," she smiled.

"So how's the play looking?" he asked.

"You know, they're kids and it's their thing," she shrugged. "Times change. I was just here to enable their vision."

"Enable," repeated Mondel.

"Yeah," she smiled. "I'll see you afterwards. Maybe we'll get a drink?"

"Yeah," agreed Mondel.

The doctor knew once he crossed the line and ruined the play, a drink was most likely out of the question. He looked around. There was a raised section of seats to the right side of the stage. Already, there was a group of reporters there "covering" the premiere of the play. Freidman was among them. He and the elite reporters from PixieRay.com, A.H. Daily, The Agenda, PNY, Populi, New Teen Trend and a whole host of other left leaning news outlets networked and chatted smugly. The cucks, dressed in waiter outfits, served them chilled champagne and expensive cheeses. They would all be writing a different story tonight, but the narrative always remained the same.

Finally, G arrived. The reporters stood in reverence as she entered. Penny, dressed in a very expensive business suit, was right by her side, as well as several more of the elite intersectionalists. A few of the trans athletes and Antifa members were on hand for security. G greeted the crowd to thunderous applause, while Mondel tried to blend in and not be noticed.

A few minutes later, the curtain rose, the lights dimmed and the audience was quiet.

"And now," said a booming voice. "Mx. Butterfly as it was meant to be performed! The right way! This play is sponsored by the Post-Binary Collective!"

Mx. Butterfly began with a speech about how the Patriarchy had always oppressed everyone, especially in Imperial America. The play now took place on the Upstate College campus, with the main character being portrayed by a genderqueer person. Each subsequent actor started every scene by announcing their gender and preferences. This seemed to delight absolutely no one and even the reporters looked bored.

After ten excruciating minutes, Mondel checked his watch. At exactly 7:13, the lights flickered and there was a commotion in the back. Mondel took his chance, as the audio visual guy rushed toward the distraction. He put the flash drive into the laptop.

A large screen dropped down behind the actors and a presentation began.

"Who is G?" said Derrick, who was doing the voice over. "She's not what she seems. She says she's trans, gender fluid or queer--- She says she's from marginalized groups, but would it surprise you to know that G is actually: Gina Whitcock, heiress to the Whitcock fortune!"

The screen image changed from a current picture of G to an older one from high school. G was a smiling, heiress with too many clothes, too much hair and jewelry. She looked like a blonde Kim Kardashian.

"Living with billionaire parents is soooo tough!" said Derrick mockingly.

Some of the Antifa guys rushed at Mondel, but he punched the first one and the others backed off. He ended up struggling with Chloe to keep the presentation rolling.

"Here she is at her prom dating a white guy! Oh, what's that? She's straight as an arrow! My-my!" said Derrick. "Guess she's not as marginalized as you think!"

The next picture featured a smashed up group of cars.

"Would it surprise you to know that she became disabled due to a drunk driving accident? An accident that her parents expunged from her record?" mocked Derrick. "Gina Whitcock or G, when are you going to check **your** privilege?"

The presentation ended and G stood up. Her followers and the reporter elite were absolutely stunned. This was much more devastating than the link Mondel had sent them. If this didn't shatter their world nothing did. Then G, with her voice shaking, spoke.

"Yes, that is me," she said. "I was born to privilege. I was a cheerleader that dated a quarterback. I had money, wealth, everything--- But I gave that up…for you."

"What?" said Mondel in disbelief.

"Like Osama Bin Laden, I struggled to get away from my rich family because Capitalism corrupts the heart and soul! The Patriarchy would've had me living in a fabulous mansion, married to a rich man--- But that's a prison I escaped! Yes, I was rich and I came here to use that wealth to help others! To help the marginalized and create equity! Who better to see the inequality of the world than a person that had so much? I realized that I am a victim too because **we're all victims**!"

There was an awkward silence. Mondel looked around. They couldn't possibly be buying this, could they? Then suddenly, the room erupted in applause. G was again surrounded by the adulation and absorbed it. Chloe, whom he was struggling with just a moment ago, was weeping and applauding. Nothing would turn her away from G. Their love for her was like his love for Upstate. He fled the auditorium to the cold.

Outside the theater, he spotted Celia packing up her car. He rushed up to her.

"Celia, hey," he said.

"Hey, Lawrence," she greeted. "Sorry, I'm getting out of here. Getting out of town too."

"You're not even going to see the end of your own play?"

"It's not my play, it's theirs," she said. "Plus I'm not down with all that Commie crap, so--- I'm done."

"Ten minutes ago you were staying," said Mondel.

"Yeah, well, woman's prerogative," she shrugged. "I'm gonna go live with this guy in Florida I know. Way warmer. And teach yoga."

"I don't understand, you're just going to move in with him?"

"Yeah, he's been pining for me for years, talks to me online," she explained.

"Are you in love with him?"

"No," she shrugged. "But he has a nice place. I'll be able to teach yoga, go to the beach. I don't need this shit anymore."

"Y-you're just--- You're just going to bail on your life like that? You just pick up and move in with a guy?" asked Mondel, not understanding.

"Yeah, why not? Wouldn't you?" she asked. "Bye, Lawrence. Be well."

Mondel watched her get in the car and drive away. It was only now that he realized the small amount of importance he played in Celia's life. He was just a convenient stop over--- Someone to keep her company while she found the most advantageous avenue toward her own goals. He was just a story for some guy in Florida.

153

Chapter 33

With nowhere else to go, Mondel snuck into the faculty building and went into his office. The place was freezing with the heat off, but he still had some whiskey left. He poured himself a belt. He looked over the books he had on the shelf for the students' benefit. He picked up Animal Farm and flipped through it. Finding the pages redacted he tossed it aside.

The doctor knew they'd be coming for him. He had betrayed they and humiliated they. They would not let it stand.

He looked out over the campus. There were fires burning inside and outside. In the distance, Tyler and Rosanna had dug out his car and were driving off campus. Students were trying to keep warm in the bitter February cold. Maybe if he could escape campus tonight he'd find the others, quit his job and join the lawsuit. But now it felt like he'd never leave the grounds.

The Antifa guys came for him. He was escorted across the frozen waste of the quad. A group of students were trying to escape campus and were stopped by the Antifa members. They looked like they were freezing.

"Please, sir! We just want to go home!" begged one student.

"Never assume gender!" roared the Antifa member, before beating the student with his baton.

The cucks were shoveling the walkways, but they could not find snow shovels. They were forced to improvise with red cups.

"C'mon, fellas!" encouraged Fawkes in a friendly, excited voice. "If we get this and two other stairwells done, we'll get a slice of bread!"

Mondel was brought into the dining hall. Even G's own troops had been reduced to eating the bulk cereals. None of the companies that did food deliveries wanted to return to campus and the dining hall was the last place with continual power. They brought Mondel into the office where the cafeteria lunch ladies organized the meals. G was waiting, holding a snifter of brandy.

154

"Leave us," she told her minions.

Mondel and G were now alone in the room.

"What are you going do?" asked Mondel. "Kill me?"

"No," laughed G, thinking the idea was ridiculous. "You're going to escape. Here. The keys to my Jetta. Enjoy."

Mondel caught them, they had a little hammer and sickle on the keychain.

"Why?" he asked.

"Because I need you, Dr. Mondel," explained G. "None of this would be possible without you. I need a face of the Patriarchy. Someone to rally the troops against and who better than Fascism Guy?"

"But you know I'm not Fascism Guy."

"It doesn't matter," she dismissed. "It is, what it is."

"You're charismatic, talented, driven--- Why use all those skills for this? Why not help people? Why not do something good?" he honestly asked.

"Have you **met** people?" she said, incredulous.

"So you don't believe in any of this? Diversity? Equality?" he asked, searching for a cause.

"People are equally weak, Dr. Mondel," she shrugged. "They're equally lame and easy to manipulate. They don't just deserve this. They **want** this."

"You're running out of food," said Mondel. "The power's going out. Soon all the pipes will freeze, people could die! Why do this?"

"Because who cares? Because life is a dull fucking pointless exercise when you have a billion dollars and parents that do nothing to stop you," she said. "I'm 19 years old and I've been to every continent on the planet. I've tasted every animal and plant there is to taste. I've had all my fuck fantasies fulfilled several times over. I've taken every drug there is. I can buy anything and do anything. But to have power? **Real** power over people? Now that's a high I cannot get just anywhere. So I am going to push this as far as it will take me. We're gonna start phase two. And if people die, well, maybe that'll be interesting. Maybe that gets my panties wet, I don't know. Because in the end, no one will stop me and if this all goes to shit, I will never, ever, ever have to take responsibility for it."

She opened the back door and guided him outside. The Jetta was at the bottom of the steps. Mondel looked back at her.

"Goodbye, Dr. Mondel," she smiled sinisterly. "You'll get your campus back soon."

Mondel drove out of the campus. The Incel Resistance, their last big move thwarted, now resorted to drive by attacks. The Antifa members engaged them by throwing milkshake cups full of quick drying cement, while the Resistance hit them with bottles.

Order was further breaking down on campus. Mondel drove the Jetta across the snowy roads until finally making it onto the highway where it was plowed.

Stunned and unsure what was real anymore, he parked G's car a few houses down on his street. At this point he wasn't sure if he could keep the vehicle or if he'd eventually be arrested for "stealing" it. He got back to his place.

"She's mentally ill," concluded Mondel. "It's the only explanation."

It was just a matter of time before her followers turned on her for not delivering the food and the equity utopia she promised. Mondel flipped on the news, hoping to hear something that might give him hope.

"Today at Reid University," said the TV anchor. "Scores of students protested the dean's handling of marginalized groups. A new branch of the Post-Binary Collective, founded in Upstate College, is demanding the same inclusive school that has been lauded in the press for weeks."

The video then cut to a shot of G with Penny standing next to her.

"Our vision of the future was attacked by racists and fascists," explained G. "But this time, on the Reid campus, our vision will finally be realized."

Mondel then understood that G would soon be leaving Upstate an empty withered husk, moving on to rot the body politick at Reid. The doctor was trapped in the most woke of places where no one would stop this spoiled teen, so long as she draped herself with the trappings of victimhood.

It was an eternity stuck in Wokeistan.

Made in United States
Orlando, FL
12 August 2022

20942541R00096